A Sea Not Full

A Sea Not Full

John Erickson

A Sea Not Full

© John Erickson 2010

This book is a work of fiction. Named locations are used fictitiously, and characters and incidents are the product of the author's imagination. Any resemblance to actual events or places or persons, living or dead, is entirely coincidental.

Published by
Lighthouse Christian Publishing
SAN 257-4330
5531 Dufferin Drive
Savage, Minnesota, 55378
United States of America

www.lighthousechristianpublishing.com

John Erickson

All the rivers run into the sea; yet the sea is not full; unto the place from whence the rivers come, thither they return again.

Ecclesiastes 1:7

Chapter 1

From where he had paddled beyond the waves, Nathan Prichard watched the relentless shore break pummel his dad on the inside of the point. He scooped up a handful of Pacific Ocean and splashed it in his face. When it came to waking up in the morning, cold salt water at dawn was better than coffee any day. He ladled another scoop into his mouth and savored the briny taste before spitting a stream back into the sea. Sixteen-year-old Nathan and his dad had surfed the place since he was a kid. He knew these waves were nothing his old man couldn't handle.

The ocean hissed, taking a breath. Waves retreated for a moment, hidden beneath a placid carpet of foam.

Nathan cupped his hands to his mouth. "Come on, Dad! Just paddle through the lull!"

When the sea fell silent, Nathan heard the familiar drone of traffic plying Highway 101. Like swarming bees, trucks piled high with lemons rolled southward along the wide Coast Highway. Their Jake brakes grumbled like some far-off artillery barrage all the way to L.A.

"Ah-ooga!" His dad bellowed his trademark war cry before plowing his longboard seaward through the frothy impact zone. Like a landing craft in retreat, he made headway towards Nathan. The rising sun squinted behind the chaparral-covered hills of Surfer's Point, struggling to warm the cobalt sea like a bloodshot eye. The Point, as locals called it, cranked out some of the best waves in Southern California. Nathan figured he couldn't ask for more: perfect waves, perfect weather, perfect everything.

His dad paddled up, a strained look on his face.

"You okay?" Nathan asked.

"Yeah." His dad sucked at the salty air like he'd just run a marathon. "Getting old I guess."

An ocean swell lifted behind them. Nathan aimed his board towards the beach and scratched to catch the wave.

"GO!" his dad commanded. "It's all yours!"

Nathan popped to his feet just as the right-breaking wave folded in on itself. Even before he looked over his shoulder, he knew his dad's eyes were fixed on him as he carved a trail across the translucent face. Although he wasn't the most patient teacher in the world, his dad had taught him all he knew about the ocean and set him on the surfer's path when he was five.

The wave reared up, arching its back. Nathan sliced a crescent into its concave belly. Then he cut back and shot a plume of spray over the backside as if he were writing his signature. Nate, as his dad and friends called him, was an excellent surfer for a high school kid. He'd been told he was good enough to turn pro and had the right look to attract big- bucks endorsements. Nate was too shy to ever pose in front of a camera. No, surfing meant just hanging out with his dad and having fun.

Nearing the beach, Nate expertly kicked out of the wave and paddled back to his dad with a broad grin plastered across his face. He couldn't imagine life getting much better. "You should have taken that one!"

"Lucky I didn't snake you." His dad laughed, crow's feet smiling at the corners of his eyes. He turned seaward on the lookout for the next set. His dad rubbed his shoulder and rotated his arm like an over-the-hill relief pitcher. "Man, that aches."

"Want to head in?" Nate asked.

His dad's normally ruddy face looked pale as winter. Divorce had sucked the life out of him. In fact, it had sucked the life out of everything fun, like surfing. Since she'd left, his mom criticized his dad for taking him to The Point early on school days. She'd warned either Nate was going to flunk out of school, or his dad was going to kill himself by paddling out in the frigid water before dawn.

"No way." His dad shook his shaggy blond head. "A couple more waves and *then* we'll paddle in."

Distant Santa Cruz Island rose from the blue horizon like the Promised Land while fishing boats made headway out of Ventura Harbor. Nate and his dad shared a dream of someday owning a sailboat so they could take surfing trips to the island.

"It's your turn." Nate lifted his chin towards the open sea.

His dad nodded that look of approval only he could give.

Pride welled in Nate as he watched his dad paddle for an outside wave. He liked that people said they looked alike. Both had sandy blond hair, though his dad's was peppered with gray. Had it not been for the generation between them, they could have been brothers.

"You'd better paddle, boy. Here comes a big one!"

Nate followed him into deeper water. The biggest wave of the morning peaked and only his dad was positioned to catch it. Two quick strokes and he jumped up. His wide feet gripped the waxy bumps on the deck of his longboard. The overhead wave launched him down the line towards the beach. His dad trimmed up and rode with his "toes on the nose."

Johnny Bane, an old-school local, yelled, "WAVE OF THE DAY, JAKE!" just before duck-diving under the breaker. Like magic, Johnny emerged behind the wave with his hair slicked back like a rock star. If Jesus had been a surfer, he'd have looked like Johnny. Long bleached out hair and a face burnished smooth like a schoolyard football.

"WHOO-HOOO!" His dad hooted the international surfer's call as the wave hollowed into a green barrel. He danced up the face and pushed a stream of water over the crest. He carved a graceful line across the breaker longboard-style and surfed for over a hundred yards before finally kicking out in shallow water. Nate's dad stood next to his board. With a burly arm hooked over his head, he pointed towards the beach. This was his sign to paddle in. It was time for a quick shower and change before Nate had to go to school.

An offshore breeze smelling of sage swept the ocean's surface clean. These were ideal surfing conditions and he wished he could skip school and surf all day. Of course, that would never happen. Not with the way his dad hounded him about his grades.

Nate bobbed among four surfers who'd joined him in the line-up. Twenty-five yards up the point, he spotted Nora Nelson and her dad surfing the river mouth. The kings of Pier Pont High—football stars, all-state water polo players and Spider Hansen, the school's only professional surfer—had all been slain by Nora's beauty. To her credit, she acted like she didn't even care. And for some insane reason, she seemed to like him.

"Nate, hi!" Nora waved both hands above her head as if he couldn't see her. She paddled towards him with the fluid movement of a sea otter. Her blond hair was pulled back into a long wet ponytail. In the early morning sun, water droplets sparkled like diamonds against her ginger-tanned face. She rode a swallow-tailed shortboard this morning, but Nora could paddle on a bar of soap and still look graceful.

"Hey."

For Nate, words came grudgingly, like water from a frozen spigot. And to make matters worse, Nora often left him speechless. But when he got up the guts to ask out a girl, she'd be the one.

"You coming on Wednesday?" Nora asked. She twisted a strand of golden hair and pulled it behind one ear.

"Yeah, sure."

Nate shot a quick glance at the other surfers, hoping they noticed him talking to her. Nora organized all of the youth group activities at the Surfers Church where her dad was pastor. She claimed she was a natural-born missionary and had told him once that her calling was to fish for souls in the surf. Kind of like how she caught Johnny Bane. Nate remembered the Sunday he stumbled to the front of the church. Tears streaming down his sunburned cheeks, Nora was there praying with him. Since then, Johnny hung onto his Bible like a drowning man hangs on to a rope.

"Awesome!" Nora said. "We start at seven. Snacks, Bible study and totally cool music. We're calling it '4-Days 'til Sunday.'"

Nora was always planning ways for people to get together. They were total opposites that way; Nora was outgoing and he was shy. But if it hadn't been for her, Nate wouldn't have met the few friends that he had.

Then he remembered. "Sounds fun." Nate lowered his voice. "But I forgot. I'm with my mom this week. Probably can't make it."

Since his parents' divorce, Nate lived alternating weekends with his mom. She didn't like him going out at night. If the bickering between his parents didn't drive him crazy, the tight rein she had on him would.

"That's okay. We'll meet again next week," Nora said.

"Alright then, guess I'll see you at school."

The next wave peaked so quickly Nate didn't have time to say goodbye. He ripped across the face, riding the wave just in front of the parking lot. His dad was probably already dressed, waiting to take him to school.

Nate dropped to the deck of his board and rode the whitewater into the shallows on his stomach. In front of him, four wet-suited surfers knelt in the beach break as if they were praying. Nate sensed someone was hurt and thought he recognized his dad's surfboard. He plunged from the deck of his board and stumbled across the cobblestone bottom. The group of men parted and he recognized his dad's shaggy head hanging limply to one side. Nate lunged forward half swimming then stumbling.

His toes gouged into barnacle-covered stones. He dropped his surfboard in a surge of whitewater and crawled the remaining few feet towards the huddle of men.

They administered CPR to his dad who lay face up in shallow water. His dad's longboard floated aimlessly, still attached to his ankle leash.

"Dad!" Nate choked out the words. "Daddy!"

Johnny Bane leaned over his dad. Cheeks like billows, he blew steady breaths into his dad's mouth. Every two breaths, Mo Archer, a local fireman, thrust down on his chest. Two men linked arms beneath him to keep his dad from going under.

"Get his board under him!" Mo shouted. But the whitewater rushed in, making it impossible.

Nate's world collapsed as he watched friends work desperately to save his dad's life. He knelt beside the men, wanting to help. He caught his dad's hand where it drifted in the surge and pressed it between his own. "Just breathe," he pleaded. Nate cried out in a boy's voice barely heard over the incoming tide. "Please God, save him!"

Chapter 2

Like the mammoth wave of a tsunami, bone-numbing fear washed over Nate as he watched surfers at The Point try to save his dad's life. His dad had taught him the cardinal rule of a waterman was to always help those in distress, yet the most Nate could do was hold his hand.

"On three, lift!" Mo Archer shouted directions to the four strong men who had finally managed to turn his dad's longboard into a stretcher. "Breathe him, Johnny! Someone get that leash off!" A surfer tore away the Velcro leash from around his dad's ankle. Mo directed CPR while the crew moved his dad to the beach.

"I'm on." Mo locked his hands together and pushed four rapid compressions just above Jacob's sternum. "Okay, go!" Mo directed.

Johnny moved to one side and blew two more strong breaths into Jacob's mouth, making his chest rise slightly.

Nate squeezed in next to Mo Archer to help support his dad's head as the men carried him to level sand. They stepped in unison looking like pallbearers

Nate had once seen at a military funeral. His heart drummed in his throat. Time seemed to have slowed down to a crawl. He wanted to pull the men along faster.

"Nate, you just keep helping me like you're doing," Mo said. He looked at Nate's feet, bloodied from stumbling across the cobblestones. "You okay, bud?"

Nate managed a nod.

"Put him down here. Easy now," Mo said. Following his command, each man dropped to a knee, and laid Nate's dad on the flat sand.

Nate couldn't bear watching the men continue CPR and turned away, but he never let go of his dad's hand.

Nate yanked at the neck of his wet suit, trying to catch his breath. It felt like a snake had wrapped itself around his chest and squeezed.

A fire truck and a paramedic's vehicle screamed into the parking lot.

Bystanders watched with hands clasped to their mouths as the paramedics ferried lifesaving equipment across the sand.

Then from behind, Nate felt a hand on his shoulder. He turned to see Nora's dad, Pastor Hans Nelson from their church.

"Nate, we're here for you." Hans' hand never left his shoulder. He murmured a prayer. "God bring calm, we ask in Jesus' name."

Hans seemed to know exactly what to do as he gently ushered Nate away from where the paramedics frantically worked. Nate remembered Nora telling him that her dad was a chaplain on call for emergencies in Ventura. The firefighters and police officers all knew him by name.

"Nate, where does your dad keep his truck key?" Hans' eyes leveled with his and never blinked.

Nate wanted to tell him without breaking down. He blurted, "In the pocket on his leash."

Hans moved among the emergency workers and found the key. Nate couldn't see his dad behind the flurry of the firemen's yellow jackets. When they finally loaded him onto a gurney, he caught a glimpse of his dad's feet, but lifesaving equipment covered the rest of him.

"Why don't we take your dad's truck to the hospital?" Hans' voice never faltered. He stood a head taller than Nate, looking down at him when he spoke.

Hans directed Nate up the beach through the crowd of bystanders who had gathered in the parking lot. Some cried; others patted him on the shoulder as he passed. Most looked away like he was some stricken man of sorrows.

The firemen secured the gurney in the back of the paramedics' vehicle. Soon after, a police officer stopped traffic while the truck carrying his dad raced out of the parking lot with its emergency lights flashing. The vehicle's screaming siren forced people to cover their ears, but Nate just stood watching with his mouth open.

Hans loaded their surfboards onto his dad's truck while Nate sat in the passenger seat staring blankly out of his open window at surfers still riding waves. In their world, nothing had changed. Nate's rapid breaths wanted to turn to sobs, which were right there if he allowed them to catch up. But he forced the sorrow down into his belly. He knew once he started crying, he probably wouldn't be able to stop.

Hans climbed into the driver's seat, still in his wet suit.

"You're going to make it, Nate. Just breathe deeply if you can." He reached over and pulled Nate's door shut. Hans started to draw his seat belt across his chest for him, but Nate stopped him.

"Thanks, I got it."

Nate took the buckle and managed to fasten it, even though his hands were shaking. He inhaled deeply until he could form words again.

"Where's Nora?" His own voice sounded distant, like a stranger's. At least he wasn't crying.

"I sent her home in my van." Han's voice was steady like the low hum of a box fan. Nothing seemed to shake the guy. But of course, it wasn't his dad who was dying.

"She drives?" Nora was a sophomore like him, but most kids in his class hadn't turned sixteen.

"Not yet, I asked a friend to drive her home." Hans drove out of the Surfer's Point parking lot and headed for the hospital.

Small talk with Hans seemed to keep Nate from slipping into the pit that he imagined would swallow him if he closed his eyes. Finally he asked the question that he knew would destroy him if it were true.

"Is my dad going to die?"

Hans took a moment to answer. His voice deepened to the pastoral tone that Nate had heard comfort the congregation after September 11th. "Nate, we don't know, but can I pray for your dad right now?"

"Sure," Nate said. For some reason, Nate thought he should close his eyes, but he couldn't.

Hans never looked away from the road. It was as if he had done this a million times before. He reached across the truck cab and placed a hand on Nate's shoulder.

"Lord, I call on you now for a miracle. God, we place Jake Prichard in your hands for your healing, and we ask that you work through the hands of the doctors to save him. Please calm Nate and let him know that you are in control. In Jesus' name, amen."

"Amen." Nate blew out his cheeks, exhaling a puff of air as if he were about to begin a race. "Thanks." His dad would have liked that they prayed together.

In silence, Nate gazed out the window at the familiar sights along Thompson Boulevard. Maybe this wasn't happening. It could all be a dream. He looked at his bloodied toes. He brushed sand away from the wounds only to feel the sharp sting of reality. No, he wasn't dreaming.

A few minutes later, they arrived at Seaview Hospital. Hans parked his dad's service truck near the emergency room entrance. Nate didn't know what to expect. He'd only been in the hospital once before when he had broken his arm in the sixth grade. The sidewalk from the parking lot stopped in front of two large glass doors inscribed "Seaview Hospital Emergency Room." The paramedics' truck that had rushed his dad to the hospital sat empty near the entrance with its rear doors flung open.

The emergency room doors automatically swung inward and the distinct smell of antiseptic blasted Nate's senses. Nate's heart ran scared. This place, with all its sanitized order, couldn't be good. He looked down at his feet again. Blood and sand had dried over his toes. Nate wondered if they would throw him out for getting the floor dirty.

Hans led Nate into the reception area of the emergency room. A nurse stepped from behind a counter and spoke to Hans in short, chopped words while Nate stood near a table piled high with magazines. He picked up the first magazine his hand touched and flipped nervously through the pages of *Better Homes and Gardens*, trying hard not to hear their conversation. He didn't want to know. When Hans finally looked over at Nate, his eyes indicated the worst.

Hans left the nurse's station and joined Nate. Nate one hand propped one hand against the wall for support. His legs no longer felt like his own.

"Why don't you sit down," Hans said quietly.

Nate dropped into the closest chair and hunched over his knees as if he was waiting to be put into a losing basketball game.

"The doctor said he probably went into cardiac arrest at the beach," Hans said. "Everyone tried, but they couldn't revive him."

His dad had been given a prescription to treat high cholesterol. Why couldn't he have just taken it like his doctor had said? Nate leaned back in the chair and looked at the ceiling, trying to find a way to get the tears to roll back into his eyes.

"Can I see him now?" Nate asked. "I really want to see my dad."

"Let me check," Hans said. He motioned to the nurse and she met him halfway across the room. He spoke to her again, this time placing a hand on her shoulder, like he'd done with Nate when he'd prayed with him.

The nurse picked up the telephone and spoke to someone quietly. Soon, a doctor came out of an examination room that adjoined the waiting area. His shoes were covered with cloth slippers the same hospital blue as his scrubs. He approached Hans first, shaking his hand. They obviously knew each other.

"Hello, I'm Dr. Gonzales," he said, putting a hand on Nate's shoulder. "If you'd like to see your dad, he's in there."

Gonzales' eyes seemed to feel more than he was saying. Maybe he had a kid Nate's age, but the distant courtesy that had always bugged Nate about doctors seemed to block any emotion. The guy had probably introduced families to death a million times. With a steady hand, he directed Nate towards the room that he'd just left and stopped short of the open door. "Nate, I'm sorry we couldn't save him."

"Okay," Nate croaked. He didn't require any more explanation than that. His wet suit, which was dry now, couldn't keep him from shivering. He stood up with his arms locked across his chest and padded barefoot past the nurse into the examination room.

Chapter 3

Nothing in his life could have prepared him for what he saw. His dad lay on an examination table, wet suit cut away from the waist up, exposing his chest and arms chiseled by a lifetime of working with his hands. Plastic vials from needles and tubes littered the floor beneath the table. The once strong arms that had taught Nate how to surf now lay by his sides with hands upturned as though in surrender. The disconnected life support equipment stood uselessly blinking. Nate sensed the great battle that had occurred. Surfers from the Point and the doctors and nurses had all had fought to save his dad's life, but the force releasing it was too strong. Although he'd never seen a dead body, Nate knew the presence of life had vanished from his dad forever.

"Dad?" Nate spoke as if his dad could hear him from that faraway place.

"Dad, I love you." Tears streamed down his cheeks to the corners of his mouth as if from a wound. Nate tasted the saltiness. Never could he remember having said "I love you" to his dad before.

His dad's hair was matted against his forehead, still damp from surfing, his black eyelashes tinged white from dried saltwater. On his wrist was a waterproof watch that he'd always worn when they surfed together before school. "Never late, because school can't wait," was his dad's motto. Around his neck hung an unassuming silver cross. He'd purchased it in Sayulita, Mexico, on a surfing trip they took to celebrate his fortieth birthday.

Nate laid his head on his dad's chest for a moment as if he were listening for a heartbeat. After a few seconds, he stood, wiping the tears from his eyes.

"Can you help me?" Nate asked.

Knowing what to do, Hans gently lifted his dad's head while Nate unclasped the chain from behind his neck. He put on the cross, letting it rest on the outside of his black wet suit. Then he undid the watch from his dad's wrist and put it on as well.

"Think you should call your mom?" Hans asked.

"Call her if you want." Nate never looked away from his dad's face. He felt the tendons of his neck pull tight beneath the grinding of his jaw. "I'm going to my dad's house."

"If you give me your mom's number, I'll let her know," Hans said.

"She won't come here," Nate said. "She hates hospitals and anything to do with sick people."

There was no one in the world he wanted to see less than his mom, but Nate gave Hans the number anyway.

Nate listened while Hans explained the tragedy in his ministerial voice. There was no way to tell what his mom's reactions were from this side of the conversation.

"Nate, I can make arrangements for your dad later today," Hans said. "But right now, I think you should go home and get cleaned up so that you can meet your mom when she comes for you."

Total resignation swept across Nate's face like a Pacific storm. "I can't just leave him here like this," Nate said.

"For now, the hospital will look after him."

Taking a last look, Nate squeezed his dad's shoulder. The muscles were tight like they'd always been. "Hope you like heaven," he whispered.

Hans put an arm around Nate's shoulder and guided him out of the examination room towards the exit. As they passed through the waiting area, they saw Dr. Gonzales again.

"Nate, I want a nurse to take a look at those feet before you go," he said. "The last thing you need to worry about this week is an infection."

The young nurse led Nate to a room behind her workstation where she cleaned and bandaged his wounds. Her blond hair, pinned back with silver combs, reminded him of Nora. Tears pooled in her eyes, threatening to spill out.

"I'm sorry about your dad," she said. She hugged Nate for a moment, holding him a bit longer than he expected. It was the first time since crawling out of the surf that Nate felt like someone cared. She walked him back to where Hans and the doctor stood talking.

"Nate, make sure and keep your feet clean," the doctor said. "And here." He gave Nate several blue foil packets. "Use this antibiotic until those cuts heal."

"Okay." Nate stared vacantly down at his feet, which were bandaged like he'd just come out of a war zone.

"Does your dad have any relatives in town?" Dr. Gonzales asked.

"No. My grandparents live in Idaho."

"I suppose they'll come to Ventura because of your father's death?" Dr. Gonzales said.

Of course they would! They weren't *that* old. Nate nodded, choking up at the thought of his grandparents getting the news.

Dr. Gonzales turned to Hans. "Have Jacob's next of kin call the hospital, will you?"

"I'll take care of that," Hans said.

The doctor patted Nate on the shoulder and shook hands with Hans. The doors to the emergency room swung inward and Hans and Nate walked back to his dad's truck.

As they drove the short distance from Seaview Hospital to his dad's house, Nate felt unmoored from all that he had ever known. He wanted to go back in time. It was like he'd been washed over the falls of the biggest wave and couldn't find his way to the surface.

Chapter 4

"Nate, do you have your key to the house?" Hans asked.

Nate jerked as if awakened from a bad dream. He'd been slumped in the passenger seat of his dad's truck like an old man, half in shock, half wishing this was all a dream.

"Yeah, I got a key." He reached for his pants pocket before realizing that he was still wearing his wet suit. Before going surfing that morning, he'd stuffed his clothes behind the seat of his dad's truck.

Nate reached behind the seat and found his jeans rolled into a bundle. He withdrew a key ring with two colored keys. His dad had painted them like this when he was in elementary school. One was red for his mom's and the other blue for his dad's house. Normally, he'd be embarrassed for showing the color-coded keys to anyone, but right now he didn't care.

Nate went to the front door and slid the blue key into the lock. It turned easily. His dad had frequently oiled the locks because the salty coastal air made them stick.

The last time he'd passed over this threshold, his dad had been hurrying them out so they could get to the beach on time. On alternating Mondays, Nate went to live with his mom. So Sunday night and Monday morning were always reserved for having fun. Last night, he and his dad had gone to Pepe's, their favorite restaurant, and this morning they got up early for a dawn patrol surf session, Nate's favorite time to surf.

Without warning, guilt tore through Nate's gut. He leaned against the weathered doorframe. If it hadn't been for him, his dad probably wouldn't have gone surfing this morning. If it hadn't been for him, his dad might still be alive.

He stumbled across the hardwood floor to the couch, collapsing like a boxer in his corner. *My dad died because of me*!

Nate looked up through the ajar front door to see his mom hurrying across the yard towards the house. She had lousy timing, as usual. Why had she shown up at all anyway? She was never there for him. Coming here was just a show for Pastor Hans. In fact, she was probably gloating over the fact that his dad was dead.

Hans came in from the garage and crossed the living room quickly to intercept his mom at the front door. "Hello, I'm Hans Nelson, we spoke on the phone. I'm sorry about Jacob."

Nate watched his mom extend her hand and Hans took it in both of his. Somehow he expected her to appear more motherly at a time like this, but he should've known better. She wore a short skirt and skimpy top that were out of place for the cool morning. She'd recently frosted the gray from her hair and it hung stylishly across one eye. When he was a kid, Nate remembered wishing she'd

spend as much time on him as she did primping her hair
for her boyfriends.

"I'm Tammy." She ran her fingers through her
hair, stiff from too much hair spray. "Oh god, I must look
like a mess," she said. She stomped the morning dew
from her sandals, and Nate saw her giving the small house
an appraising glance. This had been her house before
divorcing his dad. She'd wanted the house, but his dad
had fought her for it almost as hard as he'd fought for
Nate.

"Tammy, you look just fine. Nate's in the living
room." Hans stepped aside.
His mom pushed past Hans with an air of familiarity.
"Nate, oh my baby!"

She rushed into the living room and dropped onto
the couch next to him. The familiar smell of clove
cigarettes caught him. As a kid, he'd wait up for her to
return home from the bars fearing he might never see her
again. She'd eventually stumble through the front door
smelling of clove smoke and alcohol. When she pulled
him close to her thin frame, he felt the hooks go in. Nate
turned his face from hers, refusing to join in her insincere
wallowing.

Since the divorce, she'd done her best to ruin the
time that he and his dad had together. For years she'd
fought to pull him away and now it looked like she had
finally won.

"Mom, Dad's gone to be with the Lord," Nate
blurted, not knowing exactly why he had said it. He'd
heard the phrase used at church, but the words didn't
seem to describe what he'd seen at the hospital. Life was
gone from his dad's body, but where he had gone after
that, Nate had no idea.

"Sure he is, hon. Whatever you say."

Nate's fingers dug deep into the armrest of the dark leather couch until they stopped at the wooden frame beneath the padding. He hated when she patronized him and felt like smashing her face in. He and his dad had been going to the Surfers Church for five years. She had brushed the church off, telling him that the whole "God thing" was narrow-minded and his dad's idea.

Nate sat rigidly in his mom's grasp until she released him.

"What do I do now?" A feeling of abandonment washed over him. "Where am I going to live?"

"Nate honey, now you get to live with me." Her bony fingers squeezed his knee.

Didn't she get it? That was the last thing he wanted. Just staying with her part of the time had been torture. He was there to clean her house and help pay her bills. That was it. Most of the time, she was out drinking with her friends and never saw him anyway. Why was she acting like she cared now?

Hans' voice cleaved the tension.

"Nate, you don't need to worry about any changes right now," he said. "Your mom and I will help you take care of everything."

"Just do whatever…because I don't know what to do." Nate rubbed his temples, feeling like his head was about to explode. How would he ever be able to plan a funeral?

Hans reached for the phone. He dialed the church and spoke with his secretary, asking her to organize a support team for Nate and his family.

Nate tried to stand without wobbling. "I'm going to get some stuff from my room." He knew that at least for the time being, he didn't have a choice but to go with his mom.

"You go ahead," said Hans.

Nate went to the closet in his room and opened the door. He pulled out a duffel bag from beneath the mess on the floor. Today, his closet was a collection of memories. On any other day, his dad would have declared it a disaster zone. Packing the bag made Nate feel like he was abandoning his dad. He'd called this place "home" his entire life. He couldn't just leave.

His mom called from the other room, "Nate, can you come here a minute?"

Nate trudged back into the living room and saw that she was shuffling through several photographs.

"Honey," she said, "I didn't know your dad owned a boat."

"He doesn't. Can't you just leave his stuff alone!?" And without warning, tears distorted Nate's vision again. Right before they'd begun surfing that morning, his dad had told him that they would buy their sailboat this year. He'd probably started looking for one.

Nate tried to speak, but all that came out were breaths between sobs. He jerked away from his mom's touch. He didn't want her stinking sympathy.

"Do you think I should send him to school today?" Tammy asked, tossing the photos back onto the corner of his dad's desk.

Hans shook his head and said in a low whisper, "No."

"Then I guess I'll have to take the day off." Tammy pulled a cell phone from her small purse and went out on the front porch to make a call. She was a waitress at the Tidal Zone, a breakfast place on the pier. The rest of the day, she usually spent at the beach tanning her middle-aged body to something that resembled shoe leather.

Nate looked up at Hans. "Do I have to go with her?"

"Yes, you do," Hans said.

When the stream of sadness that had washed over him lost strength, Nate got to his feet and went into the bathroom to change out of his wet suit. His dad always said that things often got worse before they got better. He just couldn't imagine what worse was.

Chapter 5

The loss of his dad gnawed at Nate's heart. Then, it moved to his stomach. And when it wasn't in his stomach, it attached itself to his brain like a leech, gripping his thoughts so that all he could do was worry about being alone in the world with no one but his mom.

"Nate, we have to start calling your relatives. Who, in your dad's family, was closest to him?"

Hans stood in front of the couch where Nate sat with his mom. In his wet suit, with his hands clasped behind his back, he reminded Nate of one of the dolphin trainers at Marine World.

"My grandparents in Idaho," Nate said.

"Jacob's parents?" Hans asked.

"Yes," Nate said.

"Do you know their telephone number?"

"Not by heart, but I know where to find it," Nate said. He went to the rolltop desk where his dad had kept a small leather-bound address book for as long as Nate could remember. He rolled back the maple cover revealing a desktop covered with paperwork from his dad's electrical business. Every December, they'd used the address book when they sent out their Christmas cards.

Nate found the small book in a cubbyhole in the desk and handed it to Hans. Inside were the names and addresses of just about everybody they knew.

"You'll have to help me. I don't know how he's listed their names," Hans said, flipping through the dog-eared pages.

His mom suddenly looked uncomfortable sitting next to him. She probably didn't want to be sitting there when his grandparents got the bad news. Nate knew she thought his grandparents hated her after she'd divorced his dad. But that wasn't true. His Grandpa Jack and Grandma Louise had never said an unkind word about her, at least not in his presence.

His mom flipped open her cell phone and studied the screen like she was waiting for an important call. She punched in a number, probably her answering service. Then, she stood up from the couch and crossed the living room with the phone pasted to her ear. This was her pattern. If she pretended to be preoccupied with something else, then she wouldn't have to deal with him.

On her way out the front door, she turned to Nate. "Honey, Hans can help you call Jack and Louise. I really do have to go to work. There's no one to open the restaurant." She pulled her sunglasses down from where they were perched in her hair. Nate's mom shuffle-stepped in her short skirt across the hardwood floor and dropped to her knees in front of Nate, who hadn't moved from the couch. "Oh sweetie, I'm sorry. Don't worry, I'll call you at home in a while." She reached around his shoulders and squeezed him tight.

The muscles in Nate's arms and neck tightened.

His mom released him and backed away. She pretended to wipe away a tear that wasn't there. "Everything will be okay." She patted his knees. "Your dad is in a better place."

Nate nodded and said nothing. She looked pitiful sitting on her knees in front of him. His mom was all the family he had. He was stuck with her, a woman with the emotional capacity of a tomato.

She stood up and smoothed the front of her skirt before heading out the door.

"Are you at least going to the funeral?" Nate's voice followed her out the door, but she didn't seem to hear him. Although he tried telling himself that he didn't care what she did, the undertow of being ditched by his own mom dragged his heart down to a new depth.

"Nate, your grandparents' names are Jack and Louise?"

Hans carried the address book to the desk where he found a pad of paper and a pen.

"Yeah, in Sandpoint, Idaho."

"I found them." Hans dialed the number. He covered the receiver with the palm of his hand. "Would you like to tell them?"

Nate imagined his grandma's knees buckling when she got the news that her son had died, something like he'd seen in a movie. He knew that he had to make the call.

He put out his hand, letting Hans know that he wanted the receiver.

Hans nodded and handed him the phone.

Nate knew that it would be better to tell his Grandpa Jack first. His grandma had suffered from heart trouble recently and Nate didn't want to be the cause of her death too. Besides, his Grandpa Jack was the rock in their family. He was a Korean War veteran and had probably weathered more tragedy than anyone.

"Hello?"

His grandma's sweet voice still with a British accent after almost fifty years in the U.S. said, "This is the Prichard residence. Please leave a message. If you'd like to reach Jack on his cell, you can call..."

Nate scratched the cell number on the pad of paper. He disconnected the call, not leaving a message. Before losing his nerve, he redialed his grandpa's cell phone.

"Hello Grandpa?"

"Hello? This is Jack." It sounded like he was outside. He was probably out fixing something on their ranch.

"It's me, Nate."

"Hey Nate, I was just thinking about you. I'm taking those ATVs that you and your dad like to ride into town today. Got to put new tires on them."

"Oh." Nate sucked in a deep breath, trying to prepare himself for what he was about to say. "Where are you right now?"

"I'm hunting a field near the ranch to see if I can rustle up a few grouse, why?"

His grandpa loved to hunt and so did his dad.

"Well, I've got some bad news." Nate's throat tightened. He had to keep talking, or else he'd have to turn the phone over to Hans and he didn't want to do that. "Grandpa, Dad died this morning while we were surfing."

The phone line went silent. He imagined his grandfather, with his perpetually sunburned cheeks, standing in a field with a shotgun on his shoulder and his hunting dog, Tyler, at his feet.

"Nate—what? What do you...Nate, I..." His grandpa's voice crumbled, making him sound much older than his seventy years.

As much as he tried, Nate couldn't hold back the tears. When they finally subsided, he put the receiver back to his ear. And what he heard broke his heart all over again.

"Jacob, my son, why couldn't it have been me?"

Chapter 6

Nora went for a morning jog through her grandparents' neighborhood. The tree-covered streets looped around the old Sycamore Oaks Country Club in Camarillo. The three-mile run gave her precious time alone to go over what she was going to say to her dad when she called him.

After a quick shower, Nora picked up the telephone in her grandparents' bedroom and dialed her dad's office, waiting for someone to pick up at the Surfers Church. Occasionally he would answer his phone, but usually his secretary screened all of his incoming calls. With a congregation that numbered well over a thousand, her dad said he didn't have time to answer the phone himself.

"Good afternoon, this is the Surfers Church."

"Hi, it's Nora. Can I speak to my dad?"

"Certainly, Nora. Let me see if he's in."

Nora was put on hold and she heard the background music of a local radio station that broadcast her dad's sermons every Sunday. She pulled her mom's red-handled brush through her long hair. Her dad said he'd found it recently and thought she ought to have it.

"Hello, this is Pastor Nelson."

"Dad, it's me." Why did he always answer the phone like that when she called? Nora knew that Lori, his secretary, had told him who it was.

"Hi honey, how are you feeling today?"

"Dad, I'm fine and I want to come home. Besides that, I'm missing my club meetings at school."

She was president of the Bible Club and the Surf Rider's Club, and both had meetings this week. She thought that he'd sent her to her grandparents because she had been moping around the house depressed again. But of course, he never explained why he did anything. Take your pills and go to Grandma's—just another fine example of his shorthanded approach to parenting.

"Nora, I told you that I'd pick you up this weekend. I'm really busy at church and I've got to go out of town for a meeting this afternoon, so I won't be home tonight."

She knew he didn't trust her at home alone; he never had.

"School can wait, until you're…" He paused. "…until you're doing better. Have you been taking your medication?"

She knew he was sitting at his large oak desk in his office, looking at the only photo on an otherwise uncluttered desktop. The photograph was of her mom, Sarah, who had been gone for almost as long as she could remember. Nora had matted the photo herself in a gilded frame surrounded by angels.

"Dad, I'm taking one pill of Melieron every night, just like the doctor told me. And honestly, I'm feeling happy again. I really am."

She'd been taking the medication for a month. Nora had friends who had taken antidepressants since 7th grade, but her meds were different. The large rose-colored tablets reminded her of the antacids that her dad ate by the handful. The pills were made to dissolve quickly in her mouth and have an immediate effect. But all they had done was left her feeling tired and lifeless and she hated that. Right now she just wanted to convince her dad she was happy so she could come home.

"Nora, the medication is only temporary. It will help settle you down during the day until we figure out what's going on."

"Dad, nothing is going on. I'm feeling relaxed now."

Nora's fist thumped a rhythm on the nightstand next to her grandparents' bed. The fingernails of her right hand bit into the soft skin of her palm, drawing a trickle of blood. She'd flipped out after church last Sunday and had gotten so angry that she punched a hole through a wall. That was probably the reason he hadn't let her grandma take her to school this week.

"Good, because we don't want another episode like we had a few weeks ago. Do we?"

"Whatever you heard about me wanting to kill myself isn't true!" Nora began sobbing.

Nora had told a friend who then told another friend until finally her death wish had made its way through the Surfers Church to her dad. He'd said he was devastated to be the last to know. But she knew that he was embarrassed more than anything.

"Okay Nora, settle down. I want you to breathe and stop crying. We're going to work this out together, just you and me," he said evenly.

Between sobs, Nora breathed raggedly into the phone. She hated it when he used his pastor's voice with her. After taking a couple of deep breaths, she managed to compose herself.

"Dad, is Jake Prichard okay?" Nora had known Nate's dad, Jacob, for as long as she had known Nate. And she was sure the commotion on the beach Monday involved him, but her dad had sent her home with his friend before she could find out what happened.

"Jacob is still in the hospital, Nora. He just had a mild heart attack and he's recovering fine. I don't want you to worry about him," he said.

"Have you talked to Nate?" Nora asked.

"Yes, he seems to be handling things well. Now I've got to go, honey. I'll call you tonight. Remember Nora, God is in control."

"I know, Dad." She said goodbye and hung up the phone.

Sitting on her grandparents' bed, she hunched over her knees with her chin in her hands. She thought this must be what the Apostle Paul felt like when he was chained to a Roman prison guard. He needed to be out spreading the Gospel and visiting churches, but all he could do was pray and write letters from his prison cell. At least she had a telephone.

Her grandparents were so old-fashioned. They had one phone in the entire house and it was in their bedroom. She looked out of the window and saw them working in their garden. It was another beautiful day in boring Camarillo and she wished like crazy that she could go to the beach and surf The Point.

Whenever she had one of her episodes, he made sure to control everything. Her dad had given instructions that Nora wasn't to use the telephone unless she was calling him. Nora picked up the receiver and dialed Nate's number anyway. He'd be in school, but at least she could leave him a message.

Chapter 7

It was the day before his dad's funeral and Nate hadn't seen his mom all week. That was fine with him. Only a fool would think that she would change because his dad had died. His grandparents had arrived from Idaho and Nate was staying with them at a downtown hotel. Butch, a friend of his dad's since high school, had stopped by and invited him to go surfing.   Butch pulled his truck up in front of Nate's house on Palma Way so that he could get his wet suit and surfboard. It had only been a few days, but the house looked different somehow. In its silence, even the house seemed to be mourning his dad's death.

"I'll get my stuff," Nate said. He walked up the driveway, stepping over a week's worth of old newspapers. At the front door, he took the blue-colored key from his pocket.

The blinds were still closed and the small bungalow was dark for such a sunny day. Nothing looked disturbed, and the house smelled musty like after he and his dad had gone away on one of their surf trips. Nate went quickly through the kitchen and out to the garage.

He found his wet suit hanging from a hook, where Hans had left it to dry. Seeing his dad's longboard, Nate felt the familiar tightness in his throat creeping upwards like floodwater.

He unhitched his board from the top of his dad's truck and pulled his wet suit off its hanger. His dad's wet suit and longboard were alone now, looking like they were standing guard waiting for him to return.

From the garage, Nate heard the telephone ring. He carried his surf gear into the kitchen and picked up the phone before the answering machine took over. It was probably just someone calling to say how sorry they were that his dad had died.

"Hello?"

"Nate, hi, it's Nora." Her voice sounded oddly happy, considering the circumstances.

"Hey Nora, where have you been? Thought maybe I'd see you around." He hadn't heard from her all week.

"My dad sent me to Camarillo to be with my grandma. I guess he thought, you know, that…"

"Knew what?" Nate blurted. It was easier to be angry at Nora than face the hopelessness of his situation. And didn't he have a right to be? Besides avoiding him all week just like his mom had done, she couldn't even bring herself to say the truth—his dad was dead.

"Nate, I don't have time to talk," Nora said, "but I want to see you. Can you meet me at The Point?"

"Yeah, actually I'm leaving to go surf there right now. I'll be in the water with a friend of my dad's."

"Great, I'll see if I can get a ride, okay?" Nora said.

"Cool," Nate said. He wanted to see her, but he almost hoped that she wouldn't show. "Okay, see you at the beach." Nate hung up the phone, ignoring the red blinking light on the answering machine. He didn't have the energy to listen to more condolences.

Nate went out the front door, locking it behind him. He put his surfboard and wet suit into the back of Butch's truck and got in.

"Everything okay?" Butch asked.

"Yeah, it's cool." Nate fought the urge to spill his guts about how Nora had avoided him all week and now she couldn't even say sorry. "Hey Butch, you know my dad's longboard?"

"Yeah, it's an old Cat Classic isn't it?"

"You want it?" Nate asked.

"Naw. Your dad would want you to have that board, but thanks for asking."

They rode to The Point in silence except for the oldies station on the radio playing Billy Joel. Butch reminded Nate a lot of his dad that way. They both liked oldies, both surfed longboards and had little to say unless it was important. He liked that.

Chapter 8

"Grandma, can you drive me to the beach now?" Nora asked.

"Let me call your dad first," she said.

Nora stood outside the front door ready to go to The Point. The chances of success were always greater if her grandma called her dad when Nora wanted to do something.

She had a large beach bag slung over her shoulder. Inside was her wet suit, a towel and the incidentals that she always carried with her like sunscreen and surf wax. At sixteen, Nora knew that boys stared at her, but she never let it go to her head. Except for the Song of Solomon, the Bible didn't have much to say about a woman's beauty, so as hard as it was, Nora consciously tried giving little thought to her looks. For convenience, she kept her long mane of sun-bleached hair brushed back into a ponytail, or pinned up with silver combs. Either way, she preferred it out of her face when she surfed. The sinewy muscles in her shoulders and arms were defined from surfing and swimming almost every day since she was seven years old.

Nora's grandma stepped outside onto the front porch. "Honey, I can't get a hold of your dad. Are you sure surfing would be okay with him?" She stroked Nora's hair like she always did when she acted as a go-between with her dad.

"Of course it's okay. Besides, he's probably too busy to even care if I go to the beach." Nora crossed her arms and leaned into her grandmother's touch.

"Nora, your dad has a lot of responsibility leading a church like his."

"I know. I just wish he cared more about me than the stupid church," Nora said.

"Oh dear." She smoothed Nora's hair away from her forehead. "I'll take you to the beach, but I hope it doesn't get me in trouble with your dad." She kissed Nora on the cheek and walked back into the house. "Let me get my purse."

"Thanks Grandma." Nora picked up her surfboard from the freshly mowed grass and slung it under one arm. She walked out to the driveway and strapped the board to the roof racks of her grandmother's Toyota. The pungent aroma of sage from the surrounding hills triggered a memory of her mom like it always did. Sage must have been her mom's favorite perfume. She'd learned that's what Jesus lovers, like her mom, wore in the seventies. But like anything having to do with her mom, her dad wouldn't talk about it. Nora had a boatload of unanswered questions, but she gave up asking her dad about them a long time ago.

Nora's grandmother came out to the car with her purse and car keys in hand. "I don't think there's any harm in letting you go surfing today. You've been cooped up in the house for three days now and it's so beautiful outside."

Everyone in Nora's family knew how much she loved riding waves. In fact, her grandparents had just bought her a new surfboard for her sixteenth birthday. It was a popular girl's board decorated with multi-colored Hawaiian flowers set against a pink background. Nora had only ridden the board once since getting it. She had been hoping for a strong south swell so she could test it in some bigger surf.

The drive from Camarillo to Surfer's Point took half an hour. With Nora's pink surfboard strapped to the roof of her white Toyota sedan, Grandma Nelson fit right in at the parking lot at The Point.

Nora hopped out of the car and unhitched her board.

"Maybe I should stay here and watch you," her grandma said.

"It's cool, Grandma. Dad and I surf here all of the time. Plus, I'm meeting someone. Remember Nate Prichard, my friend from church? He couldn't go to school today, so his dad let him surf for a couple of hours," Nora said, believing herself. Actually, she had no idea why Nate wasn't in school. But knowing his dad, she was sure he had a good reason.

"I'll meet you back here at four o'clock. I guess I'll go shopping while you're out there." Grandma gazed seaward through the windshield and sighed. "I never get tired of that view."

When she turned towards Nora, her expression changed. A middle-aged man, standing next to their car, was pulling on his wet suit under a towel. As he wrestled with the resistant rubber suit, Nora and her grandma both caught a glimpse of the man's backside.

"You know dear, I think I better stay here until you find your friend." Nora's grandmother switched off the ignition.

"Sure," Nora said. But when she was about to strip off her t-shirt and change into her wet suit, she noticed her grandma's troubled look again.

"Grandma, I'm wearing a bathing suit under my clothes," Nora said, half pleading.

"It's just that I'm not used to seeing you change in public."

"I understand." But she really didn't. Her dad had surfed alone growing up and her grandma probably never said a word to him about anything. Nora stuffed her wet suit back into her beach bag and jogged to the public restroom just north of the parking lot.

After she had changed, she found the tissue where she had wrapped a single tablet of Melieron.

Nora shook the tablet free from the tissue and it flipped onto the damp floor of the public restroom.

"Dang!" The tablet rolled beneath the small sink and settled against the wall. Nora crouched down and picked it up. Toilet paper littered the floor beneath the sink. She stood up and held the tablet before her eyes, examining it for hair or whatever grossness that it might have picked up. She felt a surge of nervous energy and that was a warning sign of the mood swing to come. She blew hard on the pill and popped it into her mouth.

"Yuk!" She worked the pill around with her tongue until it softened.

Last week, Nora had self-diagnosed her mood swings on the Internet. Her dad, on the other hand, hadn't bothered getting a psychologist's opinion.

"It's just mild depression, believe me, I know," he'd said. "I counsel people at church with this condition all of the time."

But when Nora did her research online, she found her symptoms might be related to a more serious condition.

Bi-Polar Disorder is a mental condition causing extreme changes in an individual's thoughts and behavior. Their mood as well as their emotional state may swing erratically between manic "highs" and depressive "lows."

The Melieron tablet dissolved on Nora's tongue. She didn't want to think about anything right now except the surf. Anyway, as long as she could maintain control around her friends, she'd be fine.

Chapter 9

"Are you sure you don't want surf the Strand?"
Butch asked.
Nate stared at the flat sand where friends had laid out his
dad after they pulled him from the surf just a few days
ago.

"No, I'd rather surf here," Nate said. He fumbled
for his dad's silver cross that hung around his neck.
"Sooner or later, I have to…"

"It's cool," Butch said. He reached out and
squeezed Nate's shoulder.

It was about two o'clock on Thursday and Nate's
friends who usually surfed The Point were still in school.
That was a relief, because he didn't want to have to deal
with talking to them about his dad. Nate and Butch pulled
on their wet suits under towels. Surfers crowded the
parking lot because of the southern hemisphere swell that
was forecasted to peak that afternoon.

Nate never liked being the center of attention.
Surfers from The Point were bound to have read the
newspaper obituary written by Pastor Hans about his dad.
The funeral service was tomorrow and many of the locals

were sure to show up. He knew that all eyes would be on him: the grieving son. Just thinking about the funeral made his guts knot up.

"Hey Nate, sorry about your dad." A surfer that he didn't recognize stopped behind Butch's pickup truck.

"Thanks, I appreciate that. What's your name?" Nate asked.

"Danny. I worked with your dad on a few jobs. He helped me get hired at All County Electric."

Nate nodded.

"I'll see you at the service tomorrow. Surfers Church, right?"

"Yeah," Nate said. "Thanks."

Danny looked like he was getting choked up. He gave Nate a thumbs-up and returned to his car.

"Hey, we surfing or what?" Butch wiped at his eyes and cracked a smile.

"Yeah. Come on, let's paddle."

Nate and Butch walked to the top of The Point. Even though it was sunny, they wore full wet suits because the fall weather had turned cool and the ocean's temperature was steadily dropping as winter approached. They put on their leashes and waded through the shore break until they were in waist-deep water where they climbed onto their boards and paddled out to the line-up. Nate anticipated that more of his dad's friends would be surfing today. He made his way slowly towards the outside peak, easily duck diving under the incoming white water. Even though his surfboard was shorter and less buoyant, he reached the line-up before Butch.

Nate paddled to a stop about ten feet inside the pack of fifteen guys who were all waiting for the next wave. He looked for familiar faces. These guys weren't local. On a southwest swell like this one, The Point attracted surfers from all over Southern California, especially Santa Barbara.

Nate turned and paddled for the wave coming in from the horizon. He caught it cleanly and jumped to his feet. He looked to his left and sure enough a surfer was bearing down on him from the inside. Surfing etiquette determined that the guy to the inside, closest to where the wave broke, had rights to the wave. Nate kicked out as the surfer cut up the face of the wave and just missed him, purposely spraying a plume of water in his face. Nate shook it off and paddled back towards the line-up to try again. Normally, he could handle aggressive surfers, but today he just didn't have the energy to fight back.

The strong current had pushed Butch away from the main peak where the waves weren't as big. Nate knew Butch preferred surfing without the competitive vibe, so he didn't worry about him. While he waited in the crowded pack for the next wave, more surfers were getting into the water and paddling out. Nate watched as Butch caught his first wave, a smaller one, down into the cove.

After nearly twenty minutes of waiting for another wave, Nate decided to paddle in to the cobblestone beach and just watch. He never liked surfing in a crowd anyway.

His clothes were bundled in the back of Butch's truck, so he could change if he wanted to, but he decided to just hang out and watch the machine-like waves wrap in around the point. As each wave broke, a half dozen surfers would slide down the face of the breaker and fight for position until only one remained.

Nate pitched rocks into the white water as it frothed up through the cobblestones to his feet. With the exception of a few scabs, his feet seemed to be healing well without any sign of the infection that the doctor had talked about. The scars, if there were any, would be a constant reminder of the day that his dad had died.

As he watched a flock of pelicans flying low in formation over a swell, Nate tried not to think about the funeral the next day. Hans had told him all he had to do was show up. Easy for him to say.

Nate saw Nora come out of the restroom in her wet suit with a beach bag slung over her shoulder, looking beautiful like always.

"Nate, hi!" She always acted like she hadn't seen him forever.

"You made it." He was surprised that she'd shown up at all.

Before he could say anything, Nora said, "I'm going back to get my board and say goodbye to my grandma." She turned and jogged back towards her grandmother's white Toyota. How she managed to pull her hair back with one hand and twist it through an elastic hair tie while she ran was beyond Nate. But he always loved watching her ponytail bob up and down behind her.

In a moment, Nora cruised back up the path with a bright pink surfboard under her arm that he hadn't seen before. It must be a new one. Every guy she passed turned to get a better look. If she noticed them staring, Nora would meet their eyes with a steady gaze and just smile.

"Ready to paddle out?" Nora asked. She sounded as enthusiastic as ever.

"Yeah okay, actually I just got out of the water," Nate said.

"How come? Looks like there are plenty of waves to go around. See!" She pointed at a surfer ripping across the face of a head-high wave. "Hey, I need to put this somewhere," she said, holding up her beach bag. "Where's your stuff?"

"I came with my dad's friend, Butch. My clothes are in the back of his truck."

"Cool, can I leave my bag there?" Nora asked.

"Sure, Butch won't mind." Nate took her beach bag to the truck and stuffed it down into the corner of the bed alongside his clothes.

"Should we just paddle out here?" Nate asked. She must have known this was the exact spot where his dad had died just a few days ago.

"Looks good to me," Nora said.

They walked to the ocean's edge and put their leashes around their ankles. Nora pushed her new board through the incoming white water, jumped on and started paddling for the other surfers who were lined up outside of the breaking waves. But Nate never paddled out.

Why hadn't she asked him about the funeral, or how he was holding up? Nora was out in the line-up now. She was about fifty yards offshore, sitting in the pack when he decided to turn around and head for the parking lot. She could surf by herself.

Nate watched Nora catch a right-breaking wave that was well over her head. The pink board was fast and Nora dropped into a hollow section where she almost got tubed. By the time she'd kicked out of the wave, Nate had already walked up the beach and was undressing next to Butch's truck.

"Nate, wait up!"

Nora must have seen him get out of the water. She skipped across the cobblestone beach with her pink surfboard under her arm. He ignored her and started walking out of the parking lot with his dripping wet suit hung over the end of his surfboard.

"Nate, stop!"

He turned and looked in her direction, but pretended not to see her. Nora ran across the asphalt towards him, ignoring the cars looking for a parking space. Salt water dripped from her face like tears.

"Nate, come on. What's wrong?" She followed closely behind him, leaving wet footprints on the blacktop. "I thought we were going to surf together!"

Nate turned to face her. He felt anger working its way upward into his neck, then the warmth in his ears, knowing they were red as hot peppers. He stifled himself to a quiet shout. "Nora, you are so wacked!"

"What are you talking about?" she asked.

"I mean...you never even said, 'sorry'!" Nate stopped himself. He didn't like getting angry like this.

Finally seeming to understand, Nora blurted, "Oh Nate! I'm sorry about your dad. I just spaced because I was so stoked to get in the water after being cooped up at my grandparents' all week. How is he? Is he still in the hospital?" She tried blocking his way.

"How's my dad?! My dad's dead and the funeral is tomorrow!" Nate felt like he hated her.

"What did you say?" Nora took a step backwards, stumbling against a parked car. "Nate, I didn't know...that must be the reason...." Nora's eyes searched his. "And you said that you've been with my dad this week?"

"Yeah, Hans was there the morning he died, remember?" Nate looked beyond her towards the perfect line that separated the sky and the sea. He couldn't imagine why Hans would have lied to her. But the stricken look on Nora's face told him it was true. His anger began to subside a bit. "Your dad's been great, I mean, I don't know how I would've made it without him."

"That's why he sent me to my grandma's." Nora looked as if she was going to break down. "My dad lied to me. He never told me that your dad died. You have to believe me. Oh Nate, I'm sorry!" She reached out and wrapped her arms around his shoulders.

At first, his arms hung like dead weights. Then slowly, he embraced her. For a second, he was oblivious to the crowded parking lot where they stood. Suddenly, Nora loosened herself from him, her face looking like broken glass.

"We've got to get out of here," she said.

Nora's hair and then her tears left a damp spot on the front of his t-shirt. Her green eyes became larger and more beautiful beneath the wellsprings of tears. Nora's eyes searched his, and he wished he had answers.

"Where will we go? My grandparents are expecting me back," Nate said.

"I don't know. Can't we just be together? I don't want to be here when Butch gets out of the water, or he'll just take us back. I mean, he'll take you home, and then I'll be alone." She sucked in a deep breath as if she was trying to stop herself from crying. "Nate, I can't be alone right now," Nora said.

"We can go to my dad's house, no one's there. At least we can talk," Nate said. "Come on, you need to get your clothes."

Nora followed Nate back to Butch's truck where she'd left her beach bag. He decided to leave their boards in the back of the truck, thinking that Butch would probably drop them off at his grandparents' hotel room. He wasn't worried about what they would think when he didn't return. He just wanted to be with Nora.

Chapter 10

At Nate's house, Nora sat cross-legged across from him on the polished wood floor. She slid close enough that he felt the warm dew of her breath when she spoke.

"So he died on the beach that morning at The Point?"

The fading sun from the western sky filtered through the cracked blinds, leaving Nora's face half hidden.

"I guess. Right after I saw you, that's when he must have gone down."

"Sweet Jesus." She reached over and brushed his hair with her fingers, moving it away from his forehead. She looked away, trying to blink away her own tears. "Sorry."

"I feel so...." He couldn't put it into words. Nate wanted to be strong, but he could feel himself going over the falls again.

"Hopeless?" She laid a hand on his shoulder. "Alone?"

Compared to all the hands that had touched his shoulder this week, hers was the lightest.

"When my mom died, I felt that way, too," she said.

He remembered that her mom had died of cancer years ago. Nate pulled himself up onto the couch, trying to hide his face. He picked up the denim pillow where his dad's head probably lay the night before he died. He pressed his face into it trying to inhale any remnant of him. Without warning, he pitched the pillow across the room where it dropped like a deflated balloon against the bookcase.

"You know the stuff they teach us at church about dying?" Nate asked.

"Yes."

"I mean the stuff about where you go and what happens to your soul. You believe all that crap?"

Nora's dad had been pitching it to him all week, and now he'd been proven a liar.

"I do." She crawled up next to him on the leather couch. "I think that when we close our eyes for the last time, we go directly into God's presence in heaven."

"And you think my dad is there now?" Nate asked. Anger surged. She hadn't seen his dad lying there on the examination table at the hospital. He was gone forever.

Nora nodded.

"Let me guess, you think your mom is there too?"

"I know she is." A tear drifted from her cheek and fell between them. "I know it's hard for you to believe right now." She wiped her eyes. "Sometimes I think I'd rather be in heaven with my mom than here."

"Hey Nora, I'm sorry." Nate touched her face with the back of his hand. Her skin was so cool.

She laid her head against his chest, her breath hitching softly. It was hard for him to concentrate on that faraway place called heaven.

Nate's hand seemed to know what to do. With his index finger, he traced the outline of her jaw and lifted her chin to kiss her.

The telephone rang. Reflexively, Nate picked up the receiver from a table next to the couch. He immediately wished he'd let the answering machine get it.

"Is this Nate Prichard?"

"That's me." He looked at Nora and raised his eyebrows in a question.

"Name's Rob Sanger and I read about your dad in the newspaper. Hey, I'm really sorry, man."

"Thanks." Nate cleared his throat.

"I'm calling because your dad bought my sailboat a couple of weeks ago. Plan was for him to pick it up this weekend."

"Oh." Nate sat up straight on the couch. That explained the photos that his mom had found earlier in the week.

"I ran into a jam. Have to leave town sooner than expected. Do you have anyone who can sign papers and come and get the boat?"

Nate drove his voice down a couple octaves, trying to sound older. "Yeah, I can get those papers signed," Nate lied.

"Cool, I'm on 'A' dock, slip forty-seven at Western Shores Marina. When can you come by?"

"In an hour." Nate couldn't quite believe what he was hearing. "You telling me the boat is mine?"

"That's right."

Nate took a moment to process the thought that he was soon to be a sailboat owner. He heard the deep bass of Rasta music pulsating on the other end of the phone.

"See you at the dock." Nate hung up and went to his dad's desk, finding the photos of the sailboat that his mom had asked about the day his dad died. He shuffled through them, studying them beneath the light of a desk lamp. Nora leaned into him.

Nate dropped the photos back onto the desk. He nuzzled her knowing that if he kissed her, he probably wouldn't be able to stop. He wanted nothing else but to lay down with her right now, right here and let whatever happened, happen. *"Respect 'em and then protect them."* His dad had told him this on his way to his first dance at Pier Pont High his freshman year. At the time, he had no idea what it meant, but now it made sense.

He hugged her tightly and then forced himself to let go. "You should go home," Nate said. As much as he wanted to, he couldn't go down the sex road right now, especially with the pastor's daughter. "I have to go to the harbor and see a guy named Rob Sanger. Something about a sailboat my dad bought before he died. Guess it's mine." Though surprised by the revelation of the sailboat, Nate felt immune to anything resembling joy.

"A sailboat, are you kidding?! Don't you see?" Nora said. "This is our chance. We can take the boat and get away from here, go surfing, see the world, be together, you know?"

It was as if a switch had been turned on within her. She jerked at his arm, pulling him back down onto the couch next to her.

"I know, but I need to do this by myself."

Nate spoke as evenly as he could. He didn't know exactly what he wanted to do yet, but he wasn't getting Nora tangled up in it. "Your dad's been so cool to me and my grandparents."

"Screw him! He lied to me!" Nora shouted. "If you're going to run away on a boat, then I'm coming with you!" She stood in front of Nate with her hands clenched into fists.

"Who said anything about running away?" Nate's muscles tensed like he was preparing to ward off a blow. "Nora, I'm just going to go down there to look at the boat, okay? Why don't you just come down to the harbor with me," he said, trying his best to defuse her anger. He reached out for her hand, but she pulled it away.

"Are you coming back here?" Nora demanded.

Nate looked around. "Maybe."

He collected $200 in emergency cash that his dad kept stashed in a nightstand drawer. Nate went out into the garage to get his dad's longboard and an extra wet suit. He didn't know where he was going to be living after the funeral, but he didn't want to be without a board.

Nate stuffed his school backpack with a few items of clothing and the spare wet suit while Nora waited for him in the living room.

When they left the house, the western sky was a dusty pink and a light veil of fog threatened to mute the daylight that remained. Nate's eyes followed a con trail that disappeared somewhere over the Pacific. When he was a kid, his dad had told him that the jet leaving the trail was following the sun.

"Wow, I wonder if that's even possible," Nate said to himself.

"If what's possible?" Nora asked. Her voice had softened. It was as if she was a different person than just a few minutes ago. She reached out and took his hand.

"Oh, something my dad used to say about the jets that make those con trails. When I was a kid, he told me they followed the sun. And if they keep going, they'll never see it get dark," Nate said.

She gave him a soft elbow. "That's pretty good. It's almost poetic." Nora laughed and pulled him close, kissing him on the cheek.

"Think so?" He kicked a rock and it skittered across the sidewalk. He liked it when she was mellow and he especially liked it when she kissed him.

Streetlights began flickering on around the neighborhood. A light fog, called the marine layer by sailors, had drifted onshore like it did most nights. The fog had a way of diffusing the lights, so the high beams of cars that passed them along the way looked like search lights scanning the road. They walked to the harbor, Nate with a backpack and his dad's longboard under one arm, and Nora with her beach bag over one shoulder, never once letting go of his hand.

Chapter 11

Nate and Nora stood on "A" dock at Western Shores Marina admiring the polished hull of a sloop-rigged sailboat. The number forty-seven was stenciled in faded black on the slip's dock box and was visible thanks to a single yellow light at the end of the dock.

"Guess this is it." Nate knocked lightly on the hull.

Hearing nothing but the muffled sound of music, he rapped his knuckles harder.

"COME ABOARD!" yelled a boyish voice.

"Come on." Nate took Nora's hand and led the way up the dock steps onto the deck. The sailboat rocked gently as they stepped aboard.

Nate peered down the companionway steps into the cabin of *No Worries,* a thirty-five-foot sailboat. The voice that hailed them aboard belonged to a man who looked to be in his early thirties. He was dressed in faded blue jeans with holes at the knees.

"Come in. You Nate?" The guy held up a beer in one hand.

"Yeah and this is Nora," Nate said.

Nora signaled a "hello" with a little wave of her hand before following Nate below deck.

"Rob Sanger." He reached out to shake Nate's hand.

His grip felt strong and calloused.

"Sorry to hear about your dad." Rob was tanned to the soles of his feet and his eyes looked like he'd done some partying in his day. The sailboat's name seemed to fit him, though. The guy didn't appear to have a worry in the world.

Trying to sound older than sixteen, Nate spoke into the top of his fleece jacket, which was zipped up to his chin. "The funeral's tomorrow."

Rob nodded.

"Anyway, I appreciate the call," Nate said. He felt the tight feeling in his throat that if he didn't control would work its way up to his eyes and embarrass him in front of this guy that he didn't even know.

"Jacob told me how stoked you'd be about getting a boat. He said he planned to sail to Santa Cruz with you on the first trip out."

Nate listened, but on the table in front of him was a copy of the Ventura Telegram, which lay folded open to the obituaries. At the top of the page was the picture of his dad that he'd given to Pastor Hans.

Nora squeezed Nate's hand.

"We planned to sail to the island and surf the reefs," Nate said, able to compose himself. Nora gave him the confidence to go on. "So you found out about my dad because of his obituary?"

He nodded. "Thought I better call you right away." He looked away. "Seemed like the right thing to do." Rob went to a small refrigerator and pulled out another beer. "Your dad bought *No Worries* two weeks ago, said he planned to pick her up at the end of the month," Rob said. He reached for the controls of the stereo and turned down the crooning of Bob Marley.

Nate looked at Nora and she gave him a nod that she understood. His dad had bought the sailboat of their dreams and had planned to surprise him with it, but never got the chance.

"Let's go over the paperwork, because I have to get going. You bring someone to sign for you?" Rob looked at Nora.

"Thought I told you on the phone," Nate said, "I'm eighteen and can sign for myself."

"I won't argue with that," Rob replied. "Here's the deal. I have the pink slip for the sailboat and I've already signed it." He pointed out to his signature on the back of the crumpled pink title. "After you fill it out, take it to the DMV and *No Worries* is yours."

Nate put his hand to his mouth when he felt himself smile.

Nora leaned against the counter top near the sink and yawned. "Rob, mind if I sit down?" she asked.

"Sure." There was only one place to sit in the main salon. Rob rose from the cushioned settee, making room for her. He looked at Nate. "Go ahead and look around, if you like."

The sailboat's interior was neat and compact. Looking forward, a passageway led to the master cabin with an adjoining head that was closed off from the rest of the boat by two swinging doors. Aft of the kitchen area there were two bunks, one on each side of the boat, and cedar cabinets were located throughout the boat for storage.

"I designed and built everything below deck," Rob said. He rapped his knuckles against the aluminum mast that was stepped through the cabin floor into the boat's keel. "She's built for cruising."

Mahogany planking and toast-colored beams of Douglas fir gleamed under multiple coats of varnish. Nate thought it was the most beautiful thing he'd ever seen.

"Why don't I give you a rundown on how the engine works?" Rob padded barefoot up the steps into the chilly night air.

Nate followed him topside to the sailboat's wheel. The engine controls were mounted behind a large stainless steel wheel on a pedestal where a polished brass binnacle housed the compass. Rob was thorough but patient as he instructed Nate on the operation of the boat from bow to stern. Nate listened carefully, making mental notes of everything Rob said, but wished he had paper and pencil.

"Don't worry, man, you'll figure it out." Rob sucked down the last of his beer and crumpled the can. "I learned to sail by making plenty of mistakes. As long as you don't take her out of the harbor in a heavy blow, you should be fine. I'll give you my cell number in case you have any questions." Looking around the cockpit, he said, "Did I miss anything?"

"Can I leave the boat in this slip?" Nate asked.

"No, get her out of the marina as soon you can." Rob reached down and clicked on the compass light. A three hundred and sixty degree dial floated inside a clear globe. The soft blue light of the compass illuminated Rob's face, which was serious now.

"See, I ran into some financial problems. If you don't move her by the weekend, you'll have a collection agent breathing down your neck. I owe a casino in Vegas twenty grand and they're coming on Monday to collect." He ran his hand around the wheel.

"Then where do I keep her?" Nate asked.

"For now, the easiest place to anchor would be the yacht basin," Rob said, pointing towards the harbor entrance.

Nate nodded, although nothing was visible in the dark except the blinking red and green lights of the entrance buoys.

"If you motor past the harbor entrance, you'll see boats anchored behind the breakwater. It's well protected and nobody will bother you."

"What about the Vegas guys?" Nate asked.

"They're looking for me, not you. Besides, your dad signed a purchase agreement for *No Worries* before they put a lien against my boat. I'll give you a copy of everything. Don't forget, you need to move the boat this weekend. You don't want to give the Vegas dudes a chance to hassle you. They aren't nice people," Rob said.

Below deck, they found Nora lying on the settee snoring softly. A prescription bottle of pills lay on top of her surfing bag.

Rob picked up the pill bottle.

"Melieron," he read. He carefully placed the container in the top of Nora's bag. "Dude, this is powerful stuff."

"Is it legal?" Nate asked naively. He was surprised to see a bottle of pills anywhere near Nora. She'd been a leader in every school anti-drug campaign since kindergarten.

"It's just a prescription that treats depression. One of the side effects is sleepiness. It says to 'take one before bedtime.' Guess she was ready to go to sleep," Rob said.

"Can we crash here until she wakes up?" He knew that he shouldn't have brought Nora along.

"Yeah, that's cool. I planned to head south to my mom's tonight anyway." Rob went aft of the navigation table and grabbed a crate filled with his personal belongings. He hauled it topside.

"Need help?" Nate followed Rob on deck. He stuffed his hands into his pockets. A cold breeze sent the rigging clanging against the mast.

"No, thanks," replied Rob. "Hey, take care of *No Worries*, she's been good to me," Rob said. "And I hope things work out for you and Nora."

"Thanks."

The marine layer that had blanketed the harbor earlier that evening had lifted and Nate looked up the mast to the rigging above him. Inhaling deeply, he thought given the chance, he'd stay on this boat forever.

Rob hoisted his crate of belongings onto his shoulder and walked towards the gangway. When he got to the gate, he turned and whistled.

Nate jumped to the dock and jogged up to where Rob waited.

"You'll need this to get out." Rob handed Nate a dock key fastened to a floating key chain.

"Thanks." Nate shoved the key in his pocket.

Rob shook Nate's hand for the last time. "Always remember, 'Red sky at night, sailors' delight; red sky at morning, sailors take warning,'" Rob said with a quick smile.

"What's it mean?" Nate asked.

Rob laughed. "Whenever you leave the harbor, check the weather first." He pulled a thin gold chain from underneath his t-shirt. "Here, I want you to have this. It goes with the boat." He unclasped the chain from around his neck that was attached to a round amulet.

"What is it?" Nate turned the amulet over in his hand until the light above the gangway illuminated a tiny picture of a bent-kneed man carrying a small child on his shoulders. The man looked burdened, but the child he carried didn't look that heavy.

"It's a Saint Christopher medal. He's the patron saint of sailors. The dude's watched over me for a long time," Rob said.

"Won't you need this?" Nate asked.

"Naw, it's yours now. Besides, I'm going inland for a while. Good luck, Nate." He picked up his crate and walked the rest of the way to his truck whistling a Bob Marley tune.

Nate shrugged and put the amulet around his neck where it hung next to his dad's cross. He remembered praying hard for a miracle three days ago when his dad died on the beach. It didn't seem like God had been on his side lately, and Saint Christopher probably wouldn't be either.

Back aboard *No Worries*, Nate was carefully securing his dad's longboard on deck when he heard something stir the water behind the stern. He knew there were small junk fish around the docks, but this seemed bigger. He peered over the stern. In a flash, he saw a dorsal fin slice through the darkness and disappear in the direction of the harbor entrance.

"A shark in the harbor?" he said to himself. "Must be lost." Nothing seemed surprising after the past few days.

He finished what he was doing and quietly stepped down into the cabin where Nora was sleeping.

"Hey Nora, wake up." He nudged her shoulder softly, but she didn't respond. He found a sleeping bag on one of the aft bunks and covered her with it. She looked beautiful with her long straw-colored hair cascading off the settee onto the cabin floor. He reached down and ran his hand along her cheek. *"Protect her."* He heard his dad's voice.

Nate went into the small head and switched on the overhead light. He hadn't looked at himself in a mirror in quite a few days. His hair, stiff with salt water from the earlier surf session, was a spiked landscape. But what he noticed most were his eyes. They looked tired, and much older. The crease in his forehead looked permanently furrowed, reminding him of his dad's face after he'd worked a twelve-hour day as an electrician. Nate knew that his life as a carefree sixteen-year-old was over. Now he was a man with a sailboat.

He washed his face and flicked off the light. After he had stripped down to his boxer shorts, he crawled into the forward v-berth of the master cabin and covered himself with a comforter that Rob had left behind.

Nate folded his hands behind his head and looked up through the Plexiglas hatch cover. He felt the small cross and Saint Christopher medal that lay against the smooth skin of his chest. Above him, the stars shining in the dark sky seemed to rock gently above the mast with the movement of the boat. In a few minutes, Nate drifted to sleep to the musical clanging of the rigging. For the first time in days, he felt at peace. But he knew that would change, because tomorrow was his dad's funeral.

Chapter 12

Nora and Nate walked slowly back to Western Shores Marina pointing out sailboats along the way and comparing them with *No Worries*. They'd just had breakfast and Nora hadn't let go of his hand since they'd left the restaurant. Nate could smell the Coppertone sunscreen that she always wore. He walked close enough to her that the wind blew silky strands of her sun-washed hair against his cheek causing his knees to momentarily weaken. As much as he didn't want to think about it, his dad's funeral started at noon at the Surfers Church and he needed to head back to his grandparents' hotel room before then.

Nate saw a man standing by the marina office and sensed that he was the collection agent from Vegas that Rob had told him about. His white legs and floral print shirt made him stand out like one of the summer tourists who wandered the Ventura Pier. The guy was early.

The man dropped his cigarette and stepped on the butt, grinding it into the pavement. He pushed his gold-rimmed sunglasses up into hair that resembled an oil spill.

"Hey, excuse me," he said in a nasal accent that sounded like it just flew in from the opposite coast. "Either of you know Rob Sanger?"

Nate ignored him, but he could hear the guy right on their heels as they walked down the gangway.

Without missing a beat, Nora turned to the collection agent with a look of sadness that could have won an award.

"Yeah, I know Rob. Poor guy lost his dad a couple of days ago. You a relative?" Nora asked.

"Well no, I'm...uh, just here to see him about his sailboat," the man said.

"I know Rob said something about going to San Diego for his dad's funeral, but I haven't seen him in a couple of days. Can I tell him you stopped by?" Nora asked. She took a step closer to the man, blocking his way to the gate.

"No, I'll just call him later," the collection agent said. Nora turned and walked the rest of the way down the gangway to the gate that Nate was holding open.

"On second thought, do you mind if I follow you in?" The collection agent caught the gate just before it locked shut. "I'd like to just take a quick look at his boat before I-"

"Sorry, we're not allowed to let visitors on the dock without the owner of the boat. Someone stole a sailboat last week; it just disappeared one night. Apparently the poor couple that owned it lost everything." Nora yanked the gate closed behind her, leaving the guy gawking at them through the steel bars.

They walked quickly down the dock towards *No Worries*. Nate shot a glance at Nora and saw that she was ready to burst out laughing.

"That was awesome! I've never flat-out jacked a kook like that before!" Nora reached over and put her hand around Nate's waist. Pulling him close, she threw her head back, sending a wave of blond hair streaming behind her shoulders. "Woo-hoo!" she howled. "Man, did we leave that dude in the dust or what?!"

"Yeah, for about a minute. Nora, we've got to get the boat out of here. He's the guy Rob talked about and he's here early," Nate said. As far as Nate was concerned, the joke was over and they had business to attend to. He had no intention of losing the sailboat.

"Duh! Of course that was the guy from Vegas and we burned him!" Nora danced around Nate singing something that sounded like gibberish. She started tickling him and then draped herself onto his back, putting her lips up against his ear. "Natey, we burned the guy didn't we, Natey?" She spoke in a high-pitched cartoon voice.

Nate gently tried to shrug her off, but without success. Nora had pushed her hands up under his t-shirt and continued tickling him.

"What's with you, Nora? Get off of me! You want me to lose the boat? That guy's going to see us!" Nate spun around, almost throwing both of them into the water. He knew that if he really wanted to get her off his back, he could. But he didn't want to hurt her.

She jumped up and wrapped her legs, piggyback style, around his waist.

Nate's anger always rose in his ears first and he felt them burning. "Nora, stop acting crazy, or leave!"

Nora relaxed her grip and climbed down off him, looking hurt. "So you want me to leave?" she asked, her voice almost a whisper.

"Nora, I don't want you to go anywhere. I want you to stay with me, but I need you to be mellow and not fool around." He felt like he was talking to a child.

"Sorry Nate, I… I'm embarrassed. Sometimes I get excited like that and I can't control it." She brushed her hair behind her shoulders and stared down at the dock.

"That's okay. I like you no matter how you are. But it's just that right now, I need your help figuring out how to get the boat out of the marina before that guy comes down here and tries to take it."

Nate could see the repo guy still hanging around the locked gate, trying to find a way in.

He stepped aboard *No Worries* and jumped behind the steering pedestal, trying to remember the directions that Rob had given him the night before on how to start the engine. He turned the key in the ignition, but nothing happened.

Nate spoke aloud to himself. "What was it? Glow stick, glow worm, glow…." He was down on his hands and knees looking around the base of the wheel pedestal for whatever it was that he couldn't remember.

"Nate, I'll go below and look for an instruction manual." Nora disappeared down through the companionway.

"Yeah, try to find anything that says, 'diesel engine!'"

"Have you turned on the glow plug yet?" asked a voice from the dock.

Nate turned to the sound of the voice and saw a boy, about his own age, with windblown hair. He seemed to be inspecting the boat.

"What's up?" Nate asked. It appeared he was being judged stem to stern.

"Not much. My name's Brian. I'm a friend of Rob's. He asked me to check in on you guys this morning to see if you need any help getting out of the marina."

"Well," Nate replied, "I'm working on it, but I haven't been able to start the engine."

"Permission to come aboard?" Brian asked.

"Sure, come on," Nate said. It felt cool to be spoken to as the captain.

Brian looked light as a feather as he leapt onto the deck. Nate thought he'd be a good fit for one of his old shortboards.

"Did you switch on the glow plug?" Brian asked.

"That's it!" Nate shouted and stomped his foot on the deck so hard that he thought maybe he cracked it. "'The glow plug needs to warm up for a minute before turning over the ignition!'" Nate recited exactly what Rob had told him the night before and then flipped a switch. He tried the starter again and the diesel engine roared to life.

"Hey Nora!" Nate shouted down into the cabin. "We're out of here!"

Chapter 13

Below deck, Nora dug out her meds from the bottom of her surf bag. She quickly popped two pills into her mouth where the tablets dissolved on her tongue. Within minutes, they went to work rounding out the hard edge of anxiety that had dogged her all morning. Spending the night with Nate on the sailboat was going to be the end of her with her dad.

Hearing a commotion on deck, Nora poked her head up from the cabin below. She had brushed her hair and pinned it back with a silver comb inlaid with abalone shell. The Melieron was working now and she felt a smile return to her face.

"Everything okay out here?" Nora pretended to sound like a concerned adult. "Who are you?" She directed her attention to the boy standing behind the wheel with Nate.

"I'm Brian." His voice was quiet, almost like he didn't want to be heard.

Nora sensed that her staring made him nervous, but the guy was cute. "You live around here?" she asked.

"Yeah, I live here in the marina with my parents."

"That's so cool," Nora said. The medication caused her to stretch the word cool into a long relaxed "ew" sound.

Nate interrupted. "Hey, I know you two want to talk, but I've got a guy coming down here in about a minute to jack my boat. Brian, you got time to help me anchor *No Worries* in the yacht basin?"

"No problem, I'm here to help." Brian leapt to the dock and cast off the mooring lines. With sure-footed grace, he stepped back aboard before the boat had a chance to drift out of the slip. Working around Nate, he expertly guided the sailboat towards the harbor entrance.

Nora sat mesmerized by the thumping of the diesel beneath her seat. Spires of sailboat masts lined the docks on both sides of them as they motored down the breezeway of the harbor. She lifted her face to the west wind coming over the bow. The double dose of her meds flowed warmly in her veins and she felt freedom like she'd never felt before.

"Have you sailed much?" Brian asked.

Nora glowed. "Never in my life, but I've always wanted to learn."

"We're going to anchor over there." He pointed to a cluster of sailboats behind the breakwater. "You can steer if you like. Go on, it's easy." He moved aside so she could take the position behind the wheel. Nora steered a straight line down the main passageway of the harbor. She had to concentrate intently on the water so her attention wouldn't wander.

"This seems a lot like driving a car," Nora said. "Nate, look! I'm sailing!"

Nate was busy coiling dock lines on the foredeck and barely looked up.

A whale watching boat lined with gawkers passed *No Worries* dangerously close on the starboard side. Brian put a hand on the wheel, helping Nora correct her course so they didn't collide.

"Okay, you see that big red sailboat in the middle of the anchorage? We'll drop the hook just beyond it." While Nora steered, Brian pulled back on the throttle reducing the boat's speed as they approached the yacht basin.

"You should be a sailing instructor." She tried finding his eyes, but he kept them focused straight ahead.

"Actually, I taught sailing at a yacht club in the Virgin Islands last year."

"It shows, you're very good at explaining things," Nora said. A long wisp of hair fell across her face and she shook her head until it blew behind her like a streamer.

"Guess I've sailed for so long that it's easy," Brian said. He cupped his hands over his mouth. "Nate! You okay anchoring next to that red sailboat?"

Nate leaned against the mast. He gave Brian a sullen-faced thumbs-up.

"Nate, can you get the anchor ready?" Brian had to shout to be heard over the thumping of the engine. He turned to Nora. "Is it okay if Nate takes the wheel?"

"Sure." It was cool with her, but everything felt cool at the moment.

Brian went forward to help Nate with the anchor while Nora steered. In a moment, Nate made his way aft to the wheel.

"Here you go," Nora said. She smiled and moved aside so Nate could steer the sailboat.

"Okay, but you looked like you had it handled," Nate said. He took the wheel and throttled the boat back to neutral, slowing the forward momentum until the sailboat stalled. Then, he leaned into the throttle until *No Worries* inched ahead ever so slightly.

"That's good," yelled Brian. "Anchors away!" Brian released the anchor and it pulled a steady stream of clattering chain to the bottom. He secured his end of the chain to the windlass and yelled, "Give it some reverse."

The sailboat's engine clanked as Nate put the engine in gear. Nate held the wheel straight until the anchor gave a firm jerk as its flukes dug into the bottom.

"Okay, that should do it," Nate said.

"Very impressive," Nora said.

Once they were safely anchored, Brian lowered the inflatable dinghy into the water from the stern davits.

Nora thought it was goofy that the two guys stumbled over each other trying to help her into the bow of the little dinghy. Once they were settled, Nate shoved off and gave the outboard some gas. The dinghy's bow lifted out of the water as they   raced back into the harbor. Nora watched as *No Worries* was left behind, bobbing on her anchor. She wished that she could stay, but knew that she had to return home and face her dad. There was no telling how he would react to her disappearing from The Point yesterday.

Nate drove the dinghy past one dock after another of beautiful boats. When they came close to Western Shores Marina, Nate seemed to be scanning the docks.

Nora interrupted the droning of the motor. "Don't be paranoid about the Vegas dude, he's long gone."

Nate nodded, but she could tell he was annoyed.

Sticking out like an ugly duck among beauties was a blue-hulled sailboat so broken down that it looked like it might sink. Its unfurled sails draped like dirty sheets into its little cockpit. Beneath the sludge and dirt Nora could see the fine lines of what was once a beautiful racing boat.

"That's not yours, is it?" Nora asked.

"Nope, the marina owns it. See the lock and chain? She's not going anywhere." Brian pointed their attention to a heavy rusted chain threaded through a cleat on the dock. It ran up around the small boat's mast. "Guess that's what happens when you don't pay your slip rent."

"It's a sin to neglect such a beautiful little boat," Nora said. She wished she could somehow rescue it.

"After you drop me off, you can leave your dinghy at the Kuda dock." Brian pointed across the harbor towards a fleet of commercial fishing boats moored astern against an old wooden dock.

"Do I need a dock key?" Nate asked.

"No, it's where the lobster fishermen leave their boats. Your dinghy should be safe there."

Back at Western Shores Marina, Brian directed them between two docks until Nate pulled alongside a large offshore cruising sailboat.

"Thanks for the ride." Brian stepped from Nate's dinghy onto the dock. "If you ever need help with anything, just come by."

Nate gunned the outboard so hard that Nora had to grasp the bowline so she wouldn't fall overboard. He raced back towards the Kuda dock where Brian told them they could leave the dinghy.

Once the little inflatable was secured, they walked through stacks of smelly lobster traps on the commercial dock until they were on a street that skirted the harbor. She tried to hold Nate's hand like she'd done after breakfast, but he conveniently kept both hands stuffed in his front jeans pockets.

"You want to take the bus, or walk to the church?" Nate asked.

"Let's just walk, the bus will take forever." She thought the walk might help clear her head. Her meds had made her spacey and she wanted to be composed when she saw her dad at the funeral.

Nate finally allowed her to pull his arm behind her back as they crossed the street. If they cut through the city park adjacent to the harbor, they'd save time getting to the church.

"Think you'll get busted?" Nate asked.

"Oh yeah, I'll be grounded forever, but I don't care."

"Glad you came with me last night," Nate said.

Nora pulled him to a stop. She looked into his eyes, not wanting to miss the opportunity. "I love you, Nate."

She closed her eyes and moved her mouth towards his, kissing him softly on the lips. "I loved being there for you," she whispered.

"Yeah okay," he said.

She opened her eyes. Was that all he was going to say? She pushed closer wanting desperately to hear him confirm his love. She searched his eyes and saw only confusion.

"Better keep walking." He tried pulling away.

Nora didn't want to let go. Her embrace quickly turned into a bear hug.

"Nora, come on, let's not do this again. I've got to get to the church."

"Don't you love me?" Nora begged. "I ran away and spent the night with you! Can't you say you love me?" Like a wrestler, she adjusted her hold and clung to his wrists with both hands.

"Nora, okay, I love you. Now will you please let go? My dad's funeral is starting!" Nate wrenched his hands free and stumbled backwards. Looking absolutely terrified, he cut and ran. He jogged in the direction of the church, but Nora didn't follow.

At the grassy edge of a small park near the harbor, she stood with her hands hanging at her sides looking disoriented. Even though Nate was nearly a block away and still running, Nora spoke as if he was still standing next to her. "Nate, I do love you. I'm sorry," Nora said between rapid breaths. Her heart raced uncontrollably. She knew that she was having a breakdown. Even though it hurt to be rejected, Nora believed it was what she had wanted all along. She wasn't worthy of having a boyfriend like Nate. Now that he knew how weird she could become, he wouldn't want to hang around her anymore.

Nora's beach bag had fallen from her shoulder during the scuffle and the contents lay spilled on the grass. "What have I done?" Nora mumbled to herself. She dropped to her knees to collect her things.

Nora put everything back into the bag, except for the brown bottle of pills. She stared at the label; it read, "30 milligrams. Take one tablet at bedtime." Nora had taken two tablets not even an hour ago. She sat, staring at the label as if in a trance.

She was deeply ashamed for not having controlled herself around Nate and now she was alone. Perhaps if she just took one more pill, the pain would go away. Then, the memory came as it often did during the worst of times.

She was five years old and sitting in her mother's lap, slowly rocking with her. Her mother, in a bright orange headscarf, stroked her hair. Nora knew her mom's words that had haunted her forever. "I will never leave you," she said. But of course, she did. Her mom had died of breast cancer a few weeks later. And her dad, the good pastor, had shipped her off to her grandparents' house days before she died. Her dad never explained why she couldn't be there. Nora had carried the guilt of that day with her for years, always wondering if somehow her mom's death was her fault.

On her knees in the park, Nora mouthed, "I will never leave you."

Drowning now with no one to cling to, she removed the plastic cap from the small brown bottle. She shook it until several of the rose-colored ovals dropped into the palm of her left hand. She could eat the pills like candy if she wanted. Nora tossed the pill bottle aside and picked up her bottle of water. She popped three pills and chewed them up before washing them down with a gulp of water.

A tiny voice of reason alerted Nora's conscience against taking the overdose, because it would probably end her life. But a stronger desire to end the stabbing pain of guilt overpowered her will to hang on. The meds began their warm journey into her bloodstream. Her left hand loosened its grip and Nora liberated two more tablets, popping them into her mouth. She took another swig of water and washed them down.

Using her beach bag as a pillow, Nora reclined in the grass. She dropped the water bottle where she lay and drifted into a dreamlike stupor. She had three remaining tablets clenched in her fist, which rested at her side. The soft coo-cooing of a pair of doves high above in a palm tree accompanied Nora as she sang an old gospel favorite of her mom's.

"My hope is built on nothing less
than Jesus' blood and righteousness.
I dare not trust the sweetest frame
but wholly trust in Jesus' Name.
On Christ the solid Rock I stand,
All other ground is sinking sand;
All other ground is sinking sand."

Chapter 14

It took Nate all of fifteen minutes to run from the harbor park to the Surfers Church. Sweaty and out of breath, the sobering realization hit him that he had arrived at his dad's funeral. The sudden acquisition of the sailboat dropped from his mind as he swung open the doors to the sanctuary.

The Surfers Church convened in a building that had once been a warehouse for a construction company. Benches lined the makeshift sanctuary that seated five hundred people in each of two services every Sunday morning. A sound stage at the front of the assembly was outfitted with concert-sized speakers that hung from the ceiling and between them was an oversized screen to show videos. A burnished cross made from two old wooden surfboards was suspended above a podium that dominated center stage. This was where Pastor Hans preached his weekly sermons, which were broadcast by radio and cable television across Southern California.

Nate's jaw tightened as he walked past a table in the back of the sanctuary covered with photos that had been set out by his Grandma Louise earlier in the week.

There were pictures from when his dad was a baby all throughout his life up to last summer, when he and Nate had surfed in Costa Rica.

In jeans and a t-shirt, Nate wandered up the aisle feeling lost until he felt a tug at his hand.

"Nate, you're here!" His grandma stood up and hugged him until his dad's friend Butch stepped in to hug him too. Grandpa Jack looked tired, but seemed happy to see him.

Nate started to say something, but words wouldn't come.

"I spent the night at your house last night," Grandpa Jack said. He tousled Nate's hair, letting him know that he was forgiven. "Thought maybe you'd come back."

"Where have you been, Nate?" Grandma asked. Her coiffed gray hair made her look regal. She wore an ankle-length black dress with a collar that matched her hair. She tugged on his hand until he sat down next to her.

Composing himself, Nate said, "Nora and I just walked around talking. Sorry if I scared you."

Before Grandma could respond, Johnny Bane came to the stage with his acoustic guitar. He'd once toured with a band that backed up the Rolling Stones. Last time Nate had seen him, he was blowing breaths into his dad's lungs. Lungs that would never breathe again. A woman Nate knew as Karla, her tanned feet visible beneath a long white dress, stood beside Johnny. She owned the surf shop at The Point. Another took a seat at a grand piano near the rear of the stage. The service began and a hush came over those seated in the sanctuary. Johnny's scraggily hair draped over the corner of his guitar as he strummed the first chord to *Amazing Grace,* a hymn Grandma had chosen.

Grandma placed her hand over Nate's. The fair skin on top of her hand was translucent and Nate could see the delicate blue intersection of veins that disappeared under the sleeve of her dress. Nate felt a slight tremor and turned to see she was crying.

Grandpa Jack sat beside Nate on the other side, rustling the pages of his program until he found the words to the hymn.

Then he heard Grandpa's tenor join the chorus.
"Amazing grace how sweet the sound,
That saved a wretch like me!
I once was lost, but now am found;
Was blind, but now I see."

Nate and the small contingent of his family sat in the front row of the sanctuary. Behind them were at least three hundred people, all standing now and singing. Looking over his shoulder, Nate recognized some of the faces, but many he'd never seen before. He scanned the sanctuary for his mom, but he knew she wouldn't be there.

After singing two more songs, an assistant pastor came to the podium. Nate recognized him as Paul, a man in his mid-thirties, who made announcements on Sunday mornings.

"We welcome the Prichard family: Jack, Louise, Nate and others who have come today to mourn Jacob's passing," Paul said. The young pastor would lead the service, not Hans. Nate felt guilty knowing that he was probably out looking for Nora.

"We might not understand God's purpose in allowing Jacob to die right now. But to be sure, Jacob's death and his presence with Jesus in heaven are achieving God's ultimate purpose and work. Jacob died doing what he loved most, surfing with his son, Nate," Paul said.

Hearing his name, Nate's heart beat faster and he felt blood rush to his face. It seemed all eyes in the church were fixed on the back of his head.

Reading from his notes, the young pastor looked directly at Nate. "Surfing that morning didn't cause Jacob's death. No, surfing with Nate that morning was a blessing and it was the last act of love between Jacob and his son."

Hearing the young pastor's message worked like a sharp knife, cutting the bindings of guilt that had tortured Nate all week. He breathed a sigh of relief as tears welled up in his eyes.

Mo Archer and Johnny Bane came forward to say a few words about his dad. They assured Nate and his family that Jacob had died peacefully in the arms of those who knew him well and loved him.

After Butch read his funny but touching eulogy, others were invited to come to the podium to tell about the influence that Jake had had on their lives. Most of them Nate had never met.

"He helped me build a house…he loaned me the money to buy a car…Jacob taught my son to surf…he visited me in jail…he helped me when my husband died…" Each person's story had a similar ending, which was that his dad had helped many and never expected anything in return.

At the end of the hour-long service, the associate pastor called on everyone in the sanctuary to greet Nate's family in the front row of the church. Nate stood between his grandparents as row after row of those attending the funeral filed past. Some he knew by name, but many he had never seen before. His dad had somehow touched all of their lives, if only to touch them by his sudden death.

Refreshments were set up in the church courtyard and the assistant pastor encouraged people to stay.

On the walk from the sanctuary to the reception, Nate and his grandparents filed past Hans' office. The door was open and Nate saw Hans sitting across from Nora, holding her hands. They seemed to be praying.

Hans rose from his chair and moved to the door to close it. He spoke to no one in particular and said, "I'll join you in the courtyard just as soon as I finish here."

Grandpa Jack extended his hand across the threshold before Hans closed the door. "Thank you Hans, we appreciate all that you've done," Jack said.

Confused, Nate now had the urge to reach out and hug Nora whom he ran away from not even an hour ago. "Nora, I had to get to the funeral," Nate blurted. He moved towards her, but Hans blocked his way.

"Nate, I found her in a park, asleep. Do you know anything about this?" Hans looked back at Nora who was slumped in a chair with her head tilted back towards the ceiling. Her eyes were closed, but Nate guessed she was probably listening.

"I don't know… I…" he stuttered, "I guess I thought she'd be okay." He felt like a fool. He didn't know how to explain what had happened.

"Nate, you go on to the reception with your family. We can talk later." Hans nodded politely to Jack and closed the door to his office.

Once Nate and his grandparents arrived in the courtyard, the food was served. Nate, far from being sociable, found himself walking from table to table thanking people for coming to the funeral. Each person he met had something nice to say about his dad. He surprised himself when words that usually dropped from his mouth like rocks flowed easily among his dad's friends.

Nate saw Butch, sitting alone at a table.

"Hey Butch, sorry about yesterday. I didn't plan on ditching you like that."

"That's okay. You scared me a little, but I knew you could take care of yourself." Nate had been hearing his mom say the same thing since he was a little boy. It always made him feel unloved and not cared for, but when Butch said it, he felt more like a man.

"Thanks for speaking about my dad like you did."

"No problem. He was such a good…" Butch's voice trailed off and he just nodded.

"See you out in the water sometime, huh?"

"That'd be great," Butch said, taking a sip of coffee. "By the way, is the girl okay?"

"You mean Nora?" He shrugged. "Guess she's fine."

"Good. Hey, you take care of yourself." He turned away for a moment and wiped his eyes with a napkin. "Call me sometime, let me know how you're doing."

"I will." Nate bent down and hugged Butch. He knew that he wasn't going to be surfing for a while. Grandpa Jack had arranged for his dad's body to be transported back to northern Idaho where he would be buried in the cemetery near their ranch. The plan was that Nate would fly to Idaho with his grandparents for a week, and then after the burial, he would return to his mom's home in Ventura.

Later that afternoon, when most of the guests had left the reception, Grandpa Jack rounded up the family to say their last goodbyes. While his grandmother got a ride to the Santa Barbara airport with Butch, the plan was that Nate would go with Grandpa Jack to his mom's house to pick up a few things before flying to Idaho.

They were heading to Grandpa Jack's rental car in the church parking lot when Nate heard a calm voice call out to his grandfather.

"Jack, can I speak to you for a moment?" It was Hans. He approached them with Nora following closely behind.

"Thank you again for everything." Grandpa put an arm around Grandma Louise.

"You're welcome and blessings to your family for a safe return home. Please call the next time you're in Ventura," Hans said. Nora stood next to her dad, looking as if she could fall asleep on her feet. Her hands were behind her back and her hair hung loosely around her face. If he had the guts, Nate would have wrapped her in his arms and apologized for ditching her at the harbor. But he didn't.

"I wanted to let you know that Nora is going to be leaving us soon to attend a special school." Hans' words had an impersonal clipped sound, far from the melodious voice that he used in his sermons. "I'd like to apologize for the confusion that she caused yesterday. She hasn't ever taken off like that before, but in hindsight, I guess we should have expected that this might happen."

Hans glanced towards Nate, not so much looking at him, but through him. Nate knew the "special school" comment was meant for him. He wanted Nate to know he wouldn't be seeing his daughter again.

"Pastor, we're just glad everyone is safe," Grandpa Jack replied.

The last thing Nate wanted was his grandpa apologizing for him, but that's not what he did.

"Nate is coming with us to Idaho for the time being," he said. He looked over at Nate. "I've talked to his mom and she thinks that would be best for him." He put a firm hand on Nate's shoulder. "With all that's gone on during the past couple of days, your mom and I think that it might be good for you to live with us in Idaho for a while."

Nate couldn't believe what he was hearing. He dreaded the thought of living with his mom, but to be treated like a child and dragged off to Idaho with no say in the matter was even worse. "Wait a minute! What about school, and my friends?"

"We'll talk about that later," Grandpa said.

"No, how about right now." Nate squared off his shoulders. He felt the rush of blood go to his face.

Grandpa Jack drew in a deep breath and stepped past him. He turned towards Hans and Nora. "Goodbye Pastor, goodbye Nora." Then, he marched across the parking lot to the rental car. Seeing that Nate wasn't following, he barked, "Nate. We've got a plane to catch."

"Sorry Nora, I didn't want this. It's my fault." He reached for her.

Before he could he could make contact, Hans grabbed Nora by the hand and pulled her along like a child towards the church office.

Just as she disappeared inside the church, Nora turned and looked sadly over her shoulder. Raising a hand from her side, she waved weakly. "No worries, Nate, no worries."

Chapter 15

Nate stared vacantly out the window as Grandpa Jack drove him the couple of miles to his mom's house. He ground his teeth against the bitter taste of humiliation until he could taste his own blood. The events in his life were moving too fast and he needed to slow them down. Nate had traveled to Idaho with his dad every summer since he could remember, but he didn't want to live there. Besides, where would he surf? The worst part was that the move to Idaho had been decided between his grandpa and mom without ever talking to him first.

Grandpa Jack pulled the rental car to the curb in front of his mom's house. He hadn't seen her since the day his dad died. When Nate pulled his keys from his pocket, he saw the ignition key to *No Worries* hanging next to the red and blue house keys on the ring. There was still hope.

"Take your time," Grandpa said. He turned on the radio and searched for a news station. "I called Tammy, she's expecting you." His grandpa dropped a bundle of his dad's mail in his lap and began sorting it.

Nate got out of the car and walked up the driveway.

"Mom?" He hoped she wasn't there. He called out again, "Mom, you home?"

He heard the bathroom door close. "I'm in the shower, honey, be out in a minute."

Nate went to his bedroom and started collecting his things. As he pulled clothes from the hangers in his closet, his gut ached for Nora and so far as he knew, he'd never see her again. He kicked a pair of flip-flops, never worn, to the back of the closet. His mom had bought them after they'd had an argument.

Checking first that the bathroom door was closed, Nate rushed from his bedroom into the small kitchen. He opened the cupboard door where his mom kept her booze. He grabbed an unopened bottle of vodka and twisted the plastic cap free. He filled his mouth with the clear liquid and swallowed.

"Oh God!" He'd never taken a drink of the hard stuff before and he couldn't imagine taking another, but he did.

He chugged another mouthful. He replaced the cap and jogged back into his room. When he was finally able to swallow the stuff, it felt like his insides were on fire.

"How was the funeral, baby?" His mom was coming down the hall towards his room. For a split second, Nate thought he would throw the bottle against the bedroom wall. Instead, he buried it in the bottom of his duffel bag.

Irritation spiked his voice despite the vodka. "It was sad! Mom, the funeral was sad."

She stepped into the room wearing a bathrobe that looked like it was straight out of a Victoria's Secret catalog.

She kissed him on the cheek. It felt like the kiss of Judas.

Nate clamped his mouth shut, hoping she wouldn't smell the vodka. Then, his face hardened and he didn't care. She had agreed to send him off to live with his grandparents and that was the ultimate betrayal. He huffed a breath over her shoulder and she let go. "You're too old for that," he said.

"This little thing." She smoothed the red satin that barely covered her breasts. "It was a gift."

Why was she telling him this?

His mom carefully pulled off a clear shower cap and shook her hair. She ran her fingers along both sides of her head, pulling her hair behind her ears. The days were gone when she was the cutest thing on the beach. Her skin had been worn a leathery brown from too many years in the sun. She was attractive in an old-school sort of way, but the clothes that she wore often contradicted her forty-year-old body.

Nate didn't want to talk about the funeral or anything else with his mom. What he wanted was to split. "Remember Butch, from Santa Barbara?" he asked.

"Oh God, yes! How is he?" Butch was an old friend of his dad's that she'd always liked.

"I surfed with him yesterday and he said to say 'hello,'" Nate said.

"I know. Your grandpa called here last night looking for you. What happened?"

Nate went to the closet and raked the hangers across the wooden rod, looking for something to throw in his bag. "Nora and I just walked around, that's all."

"Oh, well I'm glad you're safe," she said. He was safe and that's all that ever mattered to her. She wasn't one to get into details and probably didn't care why he took off in the first place.

"Grandpa told me that you wanted me to go back to Idaho with them. Don't you want me to live with you?"

"Of course I want you to live with me, honey. But Natey honey, I think it's good you're around your grandparents for a while. Besides, you've always told me how much you liked Idaho."

All those years of battling his dad for custody and now, the truth comes out. She couldn't care less.

She walked out of his room drying her hair with a towel. "I'm working the lunch shift today, so I've got to get going. But don't leave until I have a chance to say goodbye."

So far as he was concerned, his mom had said "goodbye" to being a mom a long time ago. He continued tossing clothes into the old gym bag on top of the bottle. The clothes he normally wore were in his backpack aboard *No Worries*. From the foot of his bed, he picked up a new sweatshirt, still in its cellophane wrapping. He threw it in the gym bag. Buying him stuff—that's the closest his mom ever came to loving him.

She came out of her bedroom dressed, but with curlers in her hair. She hugged Nate, holding on to him for an extra couple of seconds. She walked him to the front door with an arm around his waist.

"You're turning into a man, Nate." Her voice cracked.

Whether her tears were sincere, Nate couldn't tell.

"Mom, I'll see you soon, okay?" He slung the gym bag over his shoulder and walked out to Grandpa Jack's car. His emotions had run dry and there was nothing sad about getting what he had wished for. He didn't have to live with his mom anymore, but it just hadn't happened the way that he thought it would.

Grandpa had the radio going and the windows rolled down. Nate opened the passenger side door and dropped onto the seat. His mom hunched down, looking in the window at him.

"Jack, is there anything else you need?" she asked.

"Not right now. We'll put him in school in a week or so after he's had time to adjust. I'll call you if I need his health records or anything signed," he said.

His mom nodded. Tears rolled down her cheeks.

Grandpa Jack reached across the seat, opened the glove box and found a small box of tissues. He handed the box to her through the window.

"Tammy, you know this will be the best thing for Nate. I'll have him call you as soon as we get home to Idaho." Grandpa started the car.

"It's for the best," she repeated. "Call me."

The vodka worked warmly in his veins to his smile. He patted his mom's hand. "Someday, you're going to regret this."

They drove north along Coast Highway to the Santa Barbara Airport. The road clung to the coastline below hills that looked like a camel's back. If Nate were going to make a run for the sailboat, he'd have to do it before he got on the plane.

Chapter 16

Dazed and a little drunk, Nate returned in his thoughts to Nora. He envisioned her lying on the settee aboard *No Worries* with her hair cascading to the floor. His mind spun in confusion. Even though their time together had ended badly, being with her had been the single most illuminating moment in a week filled with heartbreak and chaos.

Nate and Grandpa Jack arrived at the airport with time to spare. Grandma Louise had arrived before them and busied herself in the small gift shop while Nate and his grandpa unloaded the luggage from the rental car.

Nate's heart clanged like the forgotten bell on an abandoned ship. Maybe he should find a phone and call Nora. Or he could run from the airport and hitch a ride back to Ventura.

"Grandpa, I got to talk to you, man to man." Nate hoisted a suitcase from the trunk and set it on the curb.

"I'm listening," Grandpa Jack said. He strained against the weight of one of Louise's smaller suitcases.

"I'm old enough to make my own decision about going to Idaho," Nate said. He spoke to his grandfather much like he had always spoken to his dad, like they were on even terms.

Jack set the suitcase on the curb and straightened his back. He seemed to be examining Nate from head to toe. "At sixteen, you're not old enough to make decisions for yourself."

"Actually, I've been calling my own shots since my parents divorced," Nate said. Unknown to his grandpa, Nate's claim was true, but more so when he lived with his mom. Every day since second grade, Nate had gotten himself up in the morning, fixed his own meals, and gotten himself off to school. He did his own laundry, and even shopped for groceries when the refrigerator was empty.

"Nate, are you going to get on this plane with us, or not?"

Nate wasn't prepared for the question. "I don't know."

"I'm too old to stop you from doing what you want, but it seems if you have your mind set on staying, then that's what you ought to do."

Nate scowled. "I don't believe you."

Grandpa Jack rubbed his chin, just like Nate's dad used to do, and looked to the west where a jet was taking off. "When I was about your age, I ran away because I wanted to be my own man and make decisions for myself."

"How old were you?"

"Seventeen. Forged my old man's signature on the induction papers to join the army."

"How'd it turn out?"

"That's another story for another day." Grandpa put a hand on Nate's shoulder. "What would you say if I stayed on with you in Ventura for a while?" Jack asked.

"We'd live at my dad's house?"

"Yes, that's right," Grandpa Jack replied. Together they carried the bags to the check-in line for departing flights.

"You think my mom will make me live with her?" Nate asked.

"No, Tammy's already given permission for you to live with us," Jack said. "Why don't you come back to Idaho with us for a few days, so that I can get some things in order? We can return to Ventura in a week or so."

"Yeah, okay." A smile spread across Nate's face like a fog lifting off the Ventura coastline.

Grandpa Jack threw an arm around his shoulder and hugged him. "Let's get these bags checked so we don't miss that flight."

"What war did you fight in?" Nate asked.

"Korea. Come on, I'll tell you about it on the plane." Grandpa pulled the boarding passes from his jacket pocket and handed Nate his ticket.

****

"Night," said Nate. They had arrived at his grandparents' Idaho ranch a bit past midnight.

After his grandpa hobbled out of the bedroom, Nate went to the bathroom to wash up. Before crawling into bed, he opened a window, just like his dad had always done. A gush of cool air swept into the room. He found an old pair of his dad's flannel pajamas in a dresser drawer and slipped them on. At home he wore only boxer shorts to bed, but here in Idaho, pajamas made sense.

Nate climbed into the lower bunk of the bunk bed set where he and his dad had always slept when they visited.

Before switching off the bedside lamp, Nate scanned the room. A grainy photo of his dad and his pals sitting on the tailgate of a pickup was thumbtacked onto the wall next to the dresser. Nate recognized Butch, bare-chested with a full head of hair, hoisting a beer above his dad's head. Must have been taken in the 80s on a trip back to Idaho. He'd noticed the photo many times, but Nate had never bothered asking his dad about it when he was a kid. Now that he was gone, every moment of his dad's life seemed important.

Lying there, Nate heard the distant horn blasts from a freight train. He imagined the train was warning its way across a country road somewhere.

When he closed his eyes, his thoughts returned to Nora.

Chapter 17

Nora had spent fifteen minutes in the office of Dr. Asher, her dad's friend, and she'd had enough. He specialized in prescribing meds to kids, but so far all he'd done was grill her with stupid questions about her friends.

Asher sat in a high-backed leather chair behind an oversized desk. He wore an aloha shirt beneath his white lab coat. "So, tell me again why you ran away with your friend…" He glanced down at his notes. "Nate." He stroked his tanned face while scrawling notes on a legal pad. She figured anything she told him would be used against her. Nora felt sweat bead between the vinyl chair and her legs. It was hot as a sauna in the office, but Asher appeared comfortable.

"I told you. Nate's dad died and he needed to talk." Nora couldn't take her eyes off of a photograph of three teenagers posing on the beach. It sat conspicuously on a bookshelf behind Asher. She guessed they were his kids. How could they stand having him as a father?

"Nora, let's chat about your friend, Nate. Did he ask you to engage in any sexual activity?" Dr. Asher moved his pen from the corner of his mouth to the note pad. Nora imagined his notes being faxed to the Surfers Church for her dad to read.

"No! No sex, nada, nothing. We just talked and went to sleep!" Nora felt like slapping him.

"And that's why you took an overdose of your medication the next morning?"

"How do you know what I took? You weren't there," Nora said.

"Your dad told me he found you asleep in a park near the harbor. Do you normally sleep in parks during the day?"

"Do you normally practice medicine, Dr. Asher, or are you just a pill pusher?"

Asher's reputation was widely known, and Nora hoped she'd hit a nerve. The guy didn't have regular patients. The parents of kids she knew paid him cash to have him prescribe meds that most pediatricians shied away from.

Asher stopped writing. His right hand smoothed his lab coat, *Dr. Nelson Asher, M.D.* scrolled above the breast pocket. He crossed his arms and leaned back in his chair. He scowled at the ceiling. When he straightened up, his face had resumed its placid calm. "Nora, taking an overdose of your medication is serious stuff."

Nora heard a quiver in his voice. A smile crept across her face.

"Your mother would be disappointed."

"Don't you talk about her!" she said.

"I helped her, you know that don't you?" Asher spoke in a bland voice that reminded her so much of her dad that if she closed her eyes, it could have been him sitting there.

"Shut up!"

Asher had been an intern at the hospital where her mom died.

"I'm just trying to help you, Nora. Why'd you do it?"

"For your information, Dr. Asher, I was just tired from staying up late the night before so I took a nap." Nora didn't care how much she lied to this kook. She'd never tell him anything important about her life anyway.

After another thirty minutes of being lectured that her behavior was self-destructive and dangerous, Asher sent her home with a recommendation to continue taking her prescription of Melieron. Her dosage would be increased to 50 milligrams a day and he gave her a new prescription for a sleeping sedative. Asher told her that only her father could administer the meds, because now he considered her at risk for suicide.

Asher telephoned Nora's physician before she left his office and asked her pediatrician to follow up on his recommendations. He'd already told her dad that Nora should be given a complete physical examination. She knew the reason. He'd told her dad to be on the lookout for signs of cutting, a form of self-mutilation. She'd read about it online and heard secondhand that some of the Goth-types at her school had tried it. A certifiable nut-job—that's what Asher must think of her.

If her dad wanted to know what she had been doing with Nate, he could have just asked her, but he never did. He paid quacks like Asher to confirm that her problems had nothing to do with him. Her real feelings didn't matter. Why didn't her dad ever talk about why he'd shipped her off to her grandparents during the last weeks of her mom's life? Or why had he gotten rid of all of her mom's things after she died? Nora was twelve before she actually believed it was breast cancer that had killed her mom, and not something she had caused. She'd healed herself of this self-imposed guilt trip without any help from her dad.

On the drive home from Asher's office, Nora thought her dad was actually going to give her a chance to talk about her feelings.

"Nora, I know what's bothering you." Keeping his eyes on the road, he reached across the front seat of his van and placed a hand on Nora's shoulder.

Nora felt the long-suppressed need to cry well up inside her. Maybe, just maybe he'd let her talk about her feelings.

"Dad, I've wanted to ask you about mom for so long-"

"I know you're sad about Nate and all that he's been through, but he's not coming back."

Nora burst into tears. Nothing had changed. Her dad didn't have a clue about what she was feeling.

"Honey, I know it hurts to talk about it, but I want you to tell me about the night that you spent with Nate." Her dad spoke evenly. His hand never left her shoulder.

"*Nothing* happened!" She tried shrugging off his hand, but it only made him clamp his fingers more tightly around her shoulder. Nora drew her arm across her face, trying to wipe away the tears that lately appeared almost every time she talked to him. "Let go of me!"

"Nora! You have to tell me the truth! I'm not going to be embarrassed in front of the whole church again. What's it going to be this time, finding out that you're pregnant?" He withdrew his hand and slapped it against the steering wheel of the van.

Nora cried softly and didn't say anything the rest of the way home. If she'd had the courage, she would have flung herself from the van. Instead, she sat in silence, praying that her life might end somehow.

Chapter 18

Gravel crunched under their boots, making them sound like a troop of soldiers. Aspen and birch trees lined the road, their leaves a bluster of fiery red and orange. In late October, the crisp morning air smelled of hickory smoke. Nate had never visited Idaho in the fall. Grandpa Jack's two labs, Tyler and Buddy, fell in just ahead of them like sentries.

"You ever have a chance to go pheasant hunting with your dad?" Grandpa asked.

"Never, but Dad told me stories about how he used to hunt with you." He and Grandpa walked abreast of each other.

"There's a field west of town that I've been meaning to check out. Want to hunt it with me?" Jack asked.

"I've never fired a shotgun before in my life," said Nate.

"Jacob's twelve-gauge is still in the gun locker. It's yours, you know," Grandpa said.

"Did my dad like to hunt?" Nate asked.

"In the fall, he hunted almost every day before school," Grandpa replied.

"Sounds like I should try it then," Nate said.

He and his grandfather walked the half-mile to Lake Pend Oreille. The shoreline stretched for miles in both directions from where the country road bisected the huge lake. The labs, Tyler and Buddy, ran into the lake and lapped at the water like thirsty legionnaires.

"We better get going if we're going to get some pheasant." Grandpa Jack whistled once and the dogs bounded up from the beach for the walk home.

***

Nate shouldered the double-barreled shotgun and trudged ahead through the stubble field. Tyler crossed ten yards ahead of him.

"Get ready," Grandpa whispered.

Nate clicked off the safety. His heart beat in his throat.

On Grandpa's signal, Tyler flushed the brush pile ahead and a bird took off on a low trajectory.

Nate leveled the gun and fired twice in rapid succession. The bird folded its wings and dropped like dead weight into the stubble about thirty yards in front of them.

"Heck of a shot!" Grandpa Jack helped Nate reload his gun while Tyler ran in the direction of the fallen bird.

When Tyler returned, Grandpa commanded him to "drop," and the pheasant fell from his mouth. Nate reached down to pick up the bird whose wing tips were a beautiful hue of green. He tucked it into the game bag that he wore slung across his back.

Nate nodded towards the dense stubble ahead. "Okay, it's your turn."

He heard the click of Grandpa's safety.

"Hup!" Grandpa barked the command and Tyler froze. He shouldered his shotgun. "Go!"

Tyler bounded into the brush pile and three pheasant exploded skyward.

Boom! Grandpa's shotgun responded.

Nate dropped his gun and spun around. Something was scratching at his back. "Help me!" he shouted.

Grandpa clicked his safety on and set his gun down, taking care to point the muzzle away from Nate.

Nate was doing a wild-eyed dance trying to shrug off whatever was struggling against his back.

"Come over here!" Grandpa shouted.

Nate gyrated towards his grandpa.

Grandpa Jack reached inside Nate's field bag and yanked out the pheasant that Nate had just shot. One wing flapped wildly, brushing Nate's face.

"He's not quite dead!" Grandpa throttled the bird and spun it so hard Nate thought he was going to sling it across the field. "That ought to do it!" He dropped the bird at Nate's feet. "Go on, pick it up."

Nate stared at the bird. Its feathers were pulled away from the base of its skull and its head was facing in the opposite direction of its body. Nate forced himself to pick it up. Bile rose in the back of his throat, causing him to spit.

"Think we ought to head back now." Grandpa Jack put a hand on Nate's shoulder.

Nate turned and saw Tyler lying next to his grandpa's shotgun, licking the pheasant he'd just retrieved.

"Happens sometimes. They get stunned by the first shot, then come alive."

"It came back from the dead?"

"No." He shook his head.

"You think my dad could have been…"

"Not a chance." Grandpa picked up his gun. He cleared his throat. "Let's get going."

Before they left, Grandpa Jack cleared a shallow trench in the stubble with the heel of his boot. He pushed the pheasant he'd just shot into it and covered it with his boot.

Nate dropped to his knees and dug at the soft soil with his bare hands. He laid the pheasant with the wrung neck in the hole and pushed dirt over it.

They strode in silence to Grandpa Jack's jeep parked on the other side of the field. Nate pushed the thought from his mind. His dad's burial was the next day and unlike the pheasant, he would never wake up again.

Chapter 19

"Momma, look!" Five-year-old Nora proudly displayed another scalloped shell and tried tucking it into the front pocket of her sundress, but it was full. She ran ahead of her mom with the shell in hand. She stopped at a place where the ocean lapped gently at the sand to dig for a sand crab. She'd seen her dad do the same when he brought his fishing pole down to the beach. Nothing but gray sand sifted through her fingers. Losing interest, she took off running along the hard packed beach near the water's edge. Every time the ocean let out its breath, the water rushed up, covering her feet.

Soon, Nora was so far ahead of her mom all she saw were strangers. Terrified, she dropped the shell in her hand and ran back towards where she'd left her mom. Little Nora plodded heavily in deep sand, barely gaining ground. Although the rising tide had covered her footprints, she knew she was going in the right direction. She tried emptying her pockets to run faster, but every time she stopped, the figure that she thought was her mom got farther away. Nora passed people along the way hoping for a familiar smile. All she saw were empty faces. She dropped to her knees next to a forgotten sandcastle. The sea washed in around her and the sandcastle was swept away.

Nora awoke from the dream thinking she'd lost her mind. She reached for the nightstand and switched on the small lamp decorated in seashells. The meds had dulled her senses so much that she'd momentarily forgotten her mother's name.

Nora clawed for the dog-eared photo album that lay at the foot of her bed. In it were the only pictures that she had of her mom. She opened the album to the familiar photograph of Mom sitting on the beach holding her in her arms. Then, Nora remembered. "Her name was Sarah," she said to herself. She put the photo album aside and reached beneath her mattress for her journal. She used a spiral notebook that just two weeks ago had contained her biology notes. Before she started writing, she cracked her door enough to make sure that the lights were out in the rest of the house. Her dad had gone to sleep hours ago. Finding a blank page, she wrote furiously about everything and anything. As soon as a thought flashed in her mind, she scratched it into the notebook before she forgot.

The increased dosage of Melieron deadened every thought that came into her head. During the day, no single idea could gather any significance worthy enough to remember.

"The drugs are killing me. I can't remember a thing and all I want to do is sleep. Only time to think is now. Nate is gone. I'm trapped. Help me God! I'm dying here. If you love me, you'll save me. I promise I'll do right by you. Just set me free."

When she finished writing, Nora hid the spiral back under her mattress. She clicked off the lamp and opened the shades to the window next to her bed. Nora's body wanted to sleep, but she wouldn't allow it. She looked at the small clock on the nightstand: 3:30 a.m.

Sitting cross-legged on her bed, Nora stared out the window. The marine layer had drifted onshore overnight causing a dark fog to linger over Ventura. The ocean and air were indistinguishable. The streetlight in front of their condo cast muted light on the street below. She could run tonight and it would be hours before her dad found out. For every moment she forced herself to stay awake, the clearer her thoughts became. Tomorrow she would begin. Every great escape had a plan, but how?

Chapter 20

Just before sunset, they arrived at the small cemetery on a hill overlooking the big lake, Pend Oreille. It looked just like a place where his dad would want to be buried. A few long-time friends of his grandparents stood arm in arm with Nate on a hillside overlooking the lake.

"I'd like to say a few words before we say good-bye to our beloved son and dad, Jacob," Jack said. The small group tightened the circle with linked arms. Nate felt the familiar lump rise in his throat.

The sun flattened orange against the highest peaks of the Selkirk range west of the lake. The view reminded Nate of a postcard that he'd seen in the drugstore in town.

"This has been a tough week for us, losing our son. In fact it's been the hardest thing in our lives." Jack paused and looked skyward. "We want to thank you folks for supporting us like you have. We have faith that one day we'll see our boy again in heaven and for that, we're thankful."

A common voice murmured, "Amen."

Then the men in the group, including Nate, lifted his dad's casket from the back of the hearse and carried it to a platform above the open grave. Inlaid on each corner of the casket was the raised image of a sailboat.

The circle of friends linked arms again, this time next to the grave. Grandpa Jack laid a weathered hand on the polished cherry wood casket. "Jacob, God gave us forty-two wonderful years to know you and to love you and now he's taken you home." He struggled to finish. "We're grateful to have had you in our lives for as long as we did and now we give you back."

In one strained voice, those in the circle said "Amen" one last time. They remained linked together in silence. The only sound was the wind in the giant spruce trees above them. Below, the great lake reflected a glorious pink sky as the sun set behind the mountains.

Before they left, Grandpa gave the cemetery workers the nod that they could commence lowering Jacob's casket into the ground and finish their work. Nate surveyed his dad's final resting place. There was an empty plot next to the gravesite where his dad would be buried. It was then that he realized that his dad's grave was one of two probably purchased by his grandparents for themselves. Nate helped his Grandma Louise into the limousine and then climbed in beside her.

Grandma Louise handed him a clean tissue that she had in her purse. "Nate honey, it's okay to cry."

"Thanks, Grandma," Nate said, taking the tissue. Yes, he was sad to witness this last reminder that his dad was gone forever, but what made him cry was the thought that his elderly grandparents would die sooner than later.

For Nate, each day was a day closer to driving, dating, college and a long life. He could no sooner see his own death than he could see across the Pacific Ocean on a clear day. For the first time in his life, Nate realized that his grandparents were old. Jack and Louise had lived through a war, a couple bouts with cancer and now they had buried their only son. The end of their lives was as close as Santa Cruz Island was to the Ventura coast, which was close enough to see almost any day. Within a few years, maybe even before he graduated from high school, his grandparents would be gone and he would be alone in the world, again.

While final goodbyes were said through open windows of the limousine, Nate's eyes returned to the inlaid image of the sailboat on the corner of his dad's casket. Like a man seeing the rest of his life in the blink of an eye, Nate knew what he had to do. *No Worries* and Nora, they would sail together.

Chapter 21

Nora came into the living room after she'd finished her home-study work from Pier Pont High School. Her dad sat at his desk working on his sermon notes for the following Sunday.

"Dad, can you take me surfing tomorrow?" Nora asked. She had been planning to ask him for three days now. If he refused, then she would ask him to take her for a hike along the rugged seashore north of Santa Barbara. It seemed like forever, but last summer, this had been one of their favorite things to do together.

"What do you think?" He put down his sermon notes and gave her his full attention. "Dr. Asher said that you should ease back into your routine as soon as you're ready." He seemed to be giving her a say, which was odd.

"Well, I feel kind of sluggish." An understatement, considering she could barely keep her eyes open. Nora chose her words carefully. "But I think it's because I haven't been getting much exercise."

Her dad's eyes returned to his sermon. He scratched a note in the margins.

"I know the medicine is helping me, because I'm not having those sad feelings anymore."

Her dad removed his glasses and set his notes aside. "Mind if I pray for us?" he asked.

"I'd like that."

She sat down in front of him and waited for him to begin.

Her dad closed his eyes and inhaled deeply. When he opened them, he turned the pages of his Bible until he found a passage that satisfied him.

"Inspire us through Your Word, Lord. Renew our hearts as we pray." He paused, like he did on Sunday mornings in front of the church. Nora knew it was the sign to focus on his prayer to come.

His baritone voice rang out. "God says His, 'grace is sufficient' and 'made perfect in weakness.'"

She'd heard the passage a million times and knew its meaning.

He closed his Bible and reached for her hands, grasping them in his own. He prayed, "Lord, help us to accept our weaknesses and realize that they are a way that you can glorify your power through us. We are weak Lord and you are strong. Let us not depend on our own strength, but instead, let us depend only on you." Her dad waited for her to pray if she wanted to, but the room was silent, except for Nora's soft sobbing.

Despite her brokenness, Nora completed the well-worn pattern between them and began to pray. "Please God, give me strength to overcome my depression and get my life back on track. Lord, forgive me for running away from my problems. Please give me the strength to get better." She was finished. Now, the custom required that her dad close.

"Thank you Lord for your guidance; we pray these things in Jesus' name, Amen." Nora wanted to give him a look, showing him that she'd changed, but her eyes remained downcast.

"Things are going to get better, but we have to wait on God's timing." He placed a heavy hand on her shoulder. "How about tomorrow morning we go surfing? I hear there's a swell coming in."

"For real? Yeah, that sounds great! Dawn patrol?"

Her dad nodded.

Nora stood up and threw her arms around his neck, something she hadn't done in a while. She kissed his cheek. "Night, Dad."

"Goodnight, Honey," Hans said. He turned his attention back to his sermon. "Wait, shouldn't I give you something to help you sleep?"

He'd forgotten to give her the sleeping pill the night before. He apologized in the morning after he checked the record that he kept of all her doses.

Before she could answer, he went into his bedroom and returned with a small white tablet and a cup of water. All her meds were locked up since the last visit to Asher. "Here," he said.

He dropped it into her palm and she automatically popped it in her mouth. She took the cup from him.

"Thanks, Dad." Nora went into her bedroom and shut the door. She walked into her bathroom and looked in the mirror. She had never liked the way she looked in this mirror. The florescent light over the sink had a way of bringing out inconsistencies in her skin. Tonight her face looked pale and oily. Nora desperately wanted to look and feel like her old self again. Her lips began to move in silent prayer as she washed her face with cold water.

"God make me strong for what I need to do. Not in my strength, Lord, but yours." Nora stared in the mirror and stuck out her tongue. On it was the round white sleeping pill. She spit it in sink and ran the faucet until it disappeared down the drain.

Chapter 22

The night before they were to fly back to California, Grandpa Jack sat watching the evening news in the den while Nate's grandma baked in the kitchen. Grandma Louise had told Nate she preferred baking in the evening because it warmed up the house once the November chill set in.

The kitchen was the coziest place in the house when his grandma baked. And it was the place where Nate most liked to sit and talk to her. Tonight she made apple crisp. The sweet smell of brown sugar and cinnamon worked its way into his senses. He felt like he could spend the rest of his life rooted to that chair in the kitchen.

"Grandma?" Nate asked. "Did Dad have a girlfriend when he was in school?" He sat at the small kitchen table watching his grandmother twist the remaining dough into cinnamon rolls.

She powdered her cutting board with more flour. "Let me think, dear. I know there was a girl that he liked in junior high. But let's ask your grandfather." She walked through the living room and stood at the door to the den. "Jack, do you remember the name of the girl that Jacob liked for all of those years when he was in school?"

Jack turned off the TV and followed Nate's grandma back into the kitchen. "Now what's that about a girl?"

"You remember the girl Jacob was friends with in junior high, don't you?" Louise repeated.

Jack rubbed his chin, seeming to choose his words like he was drawing straws. "There was a girl named Katie Hargrove. Your dad met her riding the school bus in the fourth grade. They became pretty good friends as I remember."

"Were they just friends, or did they like each other like boyfriend and girlfriend?" Nate asked.

Louise spoke up. "I remember Katie came over almost every day after school. She'd help Jacob do his chores and then they would either ride the horses, or Jacob's motorcycle. But I think they were just friends."

Nate listened closely to his grandmother and soaked in every word that she said. He hungered for anything and everything having to do with his dad, and his grandparents were the lifeline that linked him with his dad's past.

Grandpa added quickly, "Katie was a childhood friend of Jacob's, but when he met your mom, he fell for her like a ton of bricks."

"Yeah I know he loved mom, Grandpa, but he had a girlfriend when he was a kid and I bet she was his first love," said Nate.

"He never told us how he felt about her, Nate. All we know is that she moved away with her family when Jacob was in the ninth grade." Grandpa walked to the refrigerator. He took a half gallon of milk out and poured himself a glass. "Thirsty?"

"No thanks," Nate replied. "What did Dad do when she moved away?"

"Well he moped around for a while," replied Grandma. "Eventually, he stopped talking about her."

Nate got up from the kitchen chair and hugged each of them goodnight. "Goodnight you guys."

"Turning in already?" Grandpa asked.

"Yeah, I'm going to sleep well tonight."

"That so?" said Grandpa Jack.

"Yeah, started sleeping with the window open just like Dad used to do." He walked out of the kitchen and went upstairs to his bedroom.

Nate tried falling asleep, but the aroma from his grandma's baking kept him awake. Suddenly, he jolted upright in bed. He hadn't checked his e-mail for almost two weeks. What if Nora had written him?

He stumbled downstairs, almost running into Grandpa Jack who was heading up to bed.

"You ready to go tomorrow?" Grandpa asked. "We're leaving on the noon flight."

"Yep, everything's packed. Mind if I check my e-mail?"

There was a desktop computer in the den hooked up to the Internet, but neither one of his grandparents had learned to use it with much success.

"If you know how to turn it on, it's all yours," Grandpa Jack replied.

"Thanks, talk to you in the morning."
Nate rushed downstairs to the den and found a newer-looking laptop on his grandfather's desk collecting dust. Once the modem connected the computer to the Internet,

Nate logged on to his e-mail account and watched the screen fill up with several pages of new mail, much of it junk. He scrolled down until he recognized a sender. The first was from his friend, Juan.

Nate, hey man, I'm sorry about your pop. Hope everyone in your family is doing well, especially you. When are you coming back to school?

Nate typed a quick reply telling Juan that he would be back at school in a couple of days. Then, Nate found a message from Nora. He opened it quickly.

Dear Nate, hope life's treating you okay. My dad has kept me locked up since you left. He was going to send me away to a different school, but instead, he just keeps me with him all the time, day and night. Wish I could see you. Sorry for acting like a fool the day of your dad's funeral. I'm better now, honest, and I miss you. Please write, Nora.

Nate hit the reply button, but didn't know exactly what to write. He missed Nora and he didn't care about the way she acted before the funeral. People acted weird sometimes and he didn't hold that against her. He felt a pang in his gut just thinking about how beautiful she was and how close they became in one night. Finally, he thought that he had the words right and started typing:

Nora, I want to see you too. We buried my dad here in Idaho, because this is where he grew up. I've thought a lot about you and I think that we should give it another try.
Nate

Like dropping in on a big wave, Nate committed himself to the chance that his feelings would get trounced if it didn't work out.

He hit the *SEND* button but nothing happened. A message box came up that said, *THE WEB PAGE THAT YOU HAVE REQUESTED HAS EXPIRED. TRY AGAIN.* Nate selected the button again, but got the same message. He gave up and shut down the computer.

Tomorrow, he and Grandpa Jack were returning to California. He'd tell Nora how he felt about her in person.

Nate returned to his bedroom. Before crawling into bed, he fished the bottle of vodka from his duffel bag. He poured it down the bathroom sink and hid the empty in the closet, figuring he'd dispose of it in the morning.

Nate crawled between the sheets of the bottom bunk. He felt for the St. Christopher medal around his neck. He'd since hung it on the same chain as his dad's silver cross. He closed his eyes and prayed. "God, thanks for giving me Grandma and Grandpa." It was the first time he'd prayed since his dad had died.

He rolled onto his side and closed his eyes. He envisioned the bent-kneed saint carrying the Christ child and then it made sense. The child bore the weight of the world's sin. That's why he seemed so heavy.

Chapter 23

The turbo prop's twin engines slowed as it dropped its flaps, reminding Nate of a pelican swooping in for a landing. The plane made its descent into Santa Barbara just past noon. Staring out the cabin window, Nate watched a patchwork of muted greens and sandy browns that were the strawberry fields opposite the airport. It had rained since they left Southern California two weeks ago and the chaparral that craved moisture even in the tiniest amount blanketed the hills in verdant green.

After picking up a rental car, they drove south on Highway 101 to Ventura. Just north of Ventura, Nate caught a glimpse of the surf at The Point.

"Look at those killer waves!" He pointed to the long lines of ocean swell that looked like a swath of corduroy wrapping in from the west.

"So that's what you guys call a winter swell, huh!?"

"Can you pull over here?" Nate directed his grandpa to the next off ramp. "This is where I used to hang out."

Grandpa exited the off ramp at Main Street. He pulled the rental car into a lot filled with surfers pulling on their wet suits. Once they found a space, Nate hopped out of the car and scrambled down to the rocky shoreline.

Every wave had at least one surfer carving a trail across its face. Some waves had as many as four surfers fighting for position. He yanked off his boots along with his socks, and then rolled up the bottom of each pant leg before wading into the whitewater. It felt good to get his feet back in cold salt water.

Seaward, he watched waves roll in perfect succession towards the beach. Nate heard surfers yelling at each other as they laid claim to the precious waves.

"My wave!" one yelled. "Hey kook, get off!" A surfer on a shortboard cursed loudly as he slashed his way in front of a guy riding a longboard.

"You see that?" Nate shook his head in disgust. "This isn't how I remember it."

"How do you mean?" Grandpa asked.

"Man, a couple of weeks ago I wouldn't have missed surfing a swell like this, might have even have skipped school. But I mean, look at the crowd."

For the first time in his life, Nate was seeing his local surf scene from a different perspective. Now he had Idaho to compare it with.

Jack picked up an egg-shaped stone and pitched it into the shore break. "Glad to be back?"

"Well, it's not Idaho, but yeah, I'm happy to be here," Nate said, knowing he didn't sound that convincing. "You want to head over to the house now?"

"Yes, but let's stop and get a bite to eat first. You know any place?"

"My dad and I used to go to Pepe's."

"Sounds good."

After they had eaten and picked up a few supplies, they returned to Nate's house on Palma Way.

Grandpa sorted the mail at the dining room table. He looked up from a small stack of bills he'd already opened.

"Those are yours." He pointed to several lavender-colored envelopes at the corner of the table.

"I wonder who they're from. Don't usually get much mail other than school stuff." Nate picked up the envelopes and examined the writing on the front of each one, which was from the same hand. "Probably just more sympathy cards." He feigned disinterest and disappeared into his bedroom.

"One more thing," Grandpa added, "there are several messages for you on the answering machine."

"Thanks, I'll check them out." Nate sat on the edge of the recliner and hit the button to replay the messages.

The machine took a moment to rewind.

"*Nate, hi, this is Nora. I really need to see you. Don't call me if you get this message, because I'm not supposed to be using the phone. I'll call you when I get a chance.*"

Another beep and Nora's voice was just a whisper. "*It's me again. When are you going to be home? Are you staying in Idaho, or living at your mom's house? Check your e-mail.*"

He fast-forwarded after catching the first couple of words of the ten remaining messages. All seemed to be from Nora.

"Everything okay?"

"Yeah, just friends wanting to know how I'm doing," Nate said. He sat hunched over the machine. All Nora except the last one from his grandma.

"Can you talk to me before you call her?"

"Call who?"

"Your friend Nora."

Nate tapped the erase button and stood up.

"Grandma wants you to call her," Nate said. He skulked into his bedroom, closing the door. Nora was none of his business.

Nate sat on his bed and opened each letter. She had e-mailed, called him and now sent him these desperate pleas for help. The message was the same each time: "I made a mistake, I'm trapped and I need to see you." He sensed the same desperation in the letters that he'd experienced the morning after they'd spent the night together on *No Worries*. Nate left the last letter unopened. As much as he wanted to pick up the phone and call her, he couldn't. What if he saw her and she clung to him the same way she had on the dock? Would he run from her again? He doubted he could handle it and wished his dad were there to talk.

Nate went into the living room where Grandpa Jack was sitting in the recliner watching the news.

"What's up?" Jack said.

"These letters, they're all from Nora," Nate said, dropping them onto the couch.

"So?"

"Think I should call her?" Nate asked.

Jack picked up the remote and turned off the TV. He straightened the back of the recliner and put his feet flat on the floor. He grasped the arms of the recliner and levered himself up onto stiff legs. He winced while he gingerly tried bending his knees.

"You okay?"

"Getting old is hell." Grandpa shuffled across the living room to the dining room table and leaned against it, trying to work the stiffness from each knee. "Seems like Nora is having a tough time," he said. "Know what's going on with her?"

"All I know is that her dad has kept her locked up since Dad's funeral," Nate said. "She says she's trapped."

"I don't know Nora," Grandpa said, "but I bet her dad has good reason to protect her."

"Protect her? From what! She's the one who almost jumped me when we stayed on the boat," Nate said.

"Her dad seems like a pretty good guy, wouldn't you say?

"Yeah, I guess."

"My guess is he probably wants to protect her from hurting herself," Jack said.

"You mean suicide?"

"Possibly, or from running away," Grandpa Jack said. "And what boat you talking about?"

Nate hadn't meant to say anything about the sailboat. He had asked Nora not to tell anyone about it and here he was shooting off his mouth.

"Nora and I stayed on a sailboat the night before Dad's funeral. Dad bought it before he died."

"A sailboat?" Jack grinned and shook his head. "He always wanted one when he was a kid." He cleared his throat. "You spent the night with the pastor's daughter on a boat?"

"Yeah." Nate steeled himself for a lecture.

Grandpa Jack's jaw worked under the skin. He sighed and forced a smile. "So tell me about it, I mean the boat."

"It's about thirty-two feet long with lots of wood on the inside. There's a little dinghy and it's got a really clean engine. Want to check it out with me tomorrow?" Nate asked.

"Sounds good. Always wanted to go sailing." Jack laughed.

"You know, you're a lot cooler than I thought."

"Guess I'll take that as a compliment." Grandpa continued stretching against the table. "It's been a long day for an old man like me. Think I'll go lay down."

"Anything I can do to help, maybe pick up some aspirin at the drugstore or something?"

"No thanks, got some in my bag." Grandpa Jack walked to his dad's bedroom and when he got to the door, he paused. Looking at Nate, he said, "I hope things work out between you and Nora."

"Yeah, me too." Nate shoved his hands in his pockets and stared at the floor.

When Grandpa Jack closed the bedroom door, Nate picked up the unopened letter, expecting it to be like all the others. He opened the envelope and thought what he smelled was the most wonderful thing in the world. He put his nose to the opening and breathed in. It had to be Coppertone, the sunscreen that Nora always wore. He pulled out a single leaf of paper. It was dated a week ago in Nora's handwritng:

"All the rivers run into the sea; yet the sea is not full." I found the verse in Ecclesiastes and it seems to fit the lost pieces of my life. I'm sorry for the confusion I've

caused you and I understand if you don't want to see me again. I'll always love you.

Nora

Nate felt a tiny bit of weight in the bottom of the envelope and turned it upside down on the coffee table. Out spilled a fine stream of sand and several tiny seashells. The edges were delicately scalloped. He picked up a shell between his fingertips and touched it to his tongue. It tasted salty like the ocean. Whatever fears he had about her disappeared.

Nate picked up the telephone and dialed Nora's number. He cleared his throat, preparing to speak with Hans, whom he sensed would answer the phone, but he wasn't afraid.

Then, like he'd just finished duck diving beneath a giant wave, he blew out a rush of air. The steady beep of a busy signal sounded on the other end of the line and Nate hung up the phone.

Chapter 24

"Thanks dad." Nora held out her hand to take her med. After putting it in her mouth, she expertly hid it under her tongue. When her dad went into his room to get ready for work, she routinely spit the tablet into the kitchen sink and washed it down the drain.

Nora went into her room to get ready for another day at the church office with her dad. When she looked into the mirror, she saw that her skin had returned to its previous golden brown and the muscles in her arms had become toned and taut again. Her dad had started allowing her to exercise in their small backyard. Nora struck a pose showing her biceps. She couldn't hide the renewed vibrancy that she felt. No thanks to her dad and his pills, she was making her awful situation bearable.

Later that morning, Nora walked into her dad's office at the Surfers Church.

"I'm finished cleaning the sanctuary. Any other work for me to do?" She hoped he did, but she didn't want to seem too eager.

Her dad looked up from examining the monthly spreadsheet of the church's finances. Nora knew too well the thick document that could change her dad's mood in an instant. It must have been a good month for passing the plate, because he was smiling.

"Why don't you take a break?" he said.

"Mind if I went jogging?"

"Yesterday we went surfing and today you want to go jogging? Maybe you really are getting better." He stood up and walked around his desk. Nora thought that maybe he was going to drag her to the hospital for a blood test to see if she was taking her medication. Instead, he hugged her. "Love you, Honey."

"Love you too." Nora looked past her dad's shoulder out the window behind his desk. It was another beautiful sunny day and she couldn't wait to get outside.

His eyes were like gray steel. "I want to trust you, okay? Go running as long as you stay on church property."

The church building was surrounded by ten acres consisting of the parking lot and a large lawn. She would run the perimeter of the property until she got tired.

"Dad, you can trust me." Nora slipped from his grasp and skipped out of his office. In the hallway, she whispered under her breath, "It's my life now."

A small voice responded. *It has been all along.*

***

Later that evening, when her dad's bedroom light went out, Nora waited half an hour before she snuck out of the house.

Since she no longer took the meds, she didn't sleep more than five hours a night and never in one stretch. It had occurred to her that her dad might have kept her mom's old things out in the garage and she was right. A week ago, she had found several unmarked boxes high on a garage shelf. For ten years, the only remnants of her mom were the photos of her in the old tattered album. What she found in the garage was a treasure trove of her mom's clothes, jewelry, old photos and letters.

With a pen light between her teeth, Nora pulled a cardboard box from a top shelf in the garage. It was unmarked and sealed like the others with clear packing tape. She set the box on the cold cement floor between her bare feet and quietly cut the yellowed tape using a steak knife that she'd taken from the kitchen.

From the box, she lifted a framed photograph of her mom and dad. Arms wrapped around each other, they looked to be on top of a mountain peak. Young and in love, she thought. She turned the frame over. In her mom's lovely handwriting it read, "Santa Cruz Island, August 1983." Her dad had led Nora's youth group at The Surfers Church to Joshua Tree and Yosemite National Parks on camping trips every year.

Beneath the photograph, she found the box full of her mom's clothes. She unfolded a blouse and swore she could smell the faint scent of sage perfume. Nora unpacked the box on the garage floor, resurrecting a memory of her mom that she never knew existed.

She tried on the blouse and a white cotton skirt. She posed in front of a dimly lit mirror with only the tiny flashlight illuminating her reflection. Like a song, her voice rose above a whisper. "Hey Nate, what do you think?" She giggled and threw her head back, blond hair cascading behind her shoulders.

Nora slipped on a pair of leather sandals that still had sand dried to the bottoms. Below the clothing, she found a tan leather bag tied closed with yellow ribbon. Inside were several pieces of jewelry. Among the shell earrings and polished stone rings was a small silver cross on a matching necklace. It was too beautiful to leave behind, so she slid it into her pocket. She thought maybe she'd find her mom's wedding ring, but it wasn't there.

Nora repacked everything as she had found it, and then returned the box to the garage shelf.

It was nearly 2 a.m. Nora reached beneath the mattress for her spiral notebook. The last thing she did was make notes of the wonderful treasures she had found.

Nora awoke the next morning to someone knocking at the front door of their condo. She pulled on a pair of shorts under the oversized t-shirt that she wore instead of pajamas. She ran a brush through her hair and twisted it into a quick ponytail. After rinsing the sleep from her eyes, she went into the living room to see who it was.

Whomever her dad was talking to at the front door wasn't invited in. He spoke in his pastoral tone but sounded irritated.

"Hope we see you back at church, Nate," her dad said.

Nora's heart skipped a beat. What was Nate doing here? She looked out from behind the blinds in the living room. Nate stood on their front porch.

She pushed past her dad who blocked the doorway. "Hey Nate, what's up?" She wanted to control the fear in her voice.

Her dad's melodious tone changed to that of a drill instructor. "Nora! Get inside!" He caught her by the arm before she got off the front porch and spun her backwards into the house.

"Just give me a minute to talk to her." Nate stood his ground, unafraid. Most people were so intimidated by her dad they'd be running by now.

"Nate, go on home." He stepped back into the house, letting the screen door close in front of him. Nate leapt onto the porch and managed to block the aluminum door open with his foot.

"I said, go home!" Her dad gave Nate a push that sent him hurtling backwards off the porch.

"Dad! Leave him alone!" Nora ducked beneath her dad's outstretched arm. She jumped from the porch and dropped to her knees next to Nate. The grass was wet with dew.

Nate took her hand. "I'm okay."

His touch calmed her for just a moment.

Nora looked up. She'd never seen her dad look so angry. With fists balled at his sides, he looked like he was winding up to kick Nate off the lawn. He grabbed Nora by the arm.

"Get inside, I tell you!" Her dad's face was red and his eyes bulged.

"Hans, let her go!" Nate got to his feet. The freshly cut grass stuck to his jeans.

Nora was crying as her dad shoved her into the house. He slammed the screen door closed and wheeled around to face Nate.

"Hans, I'll leave, okay? But I just need to say something first." Nate held his open hands in front of him like he was ready to ward off a blow. His feet were set in wrestler's stance one behind the other, but his face remained completely calm.

"What is it?"

"You helped me through the death of my dad and I don't know how I would've gotten by without you."

From behind the screen door, Nora watched her dad take a deep breath and unclench his fists.

"Nora loves you, man; you're all she's got." Nate seemed to be speaking from a place in his heart that wasn't entirely his own. He seemed to have the courage to tell her dad what she couldn't.

"Hans, I don't know exactly what's going on between you two, but whatever it is, it's killing her." Nate gazed skyward and blew out a gust of air. "I can't explain it. Just like you were there for me the morning my dad died, I got up this morning and knew that I needed to be here for Nora."

Looking down, Nate brushed clumps of wet grass from his jeans. He didn't say anything, not even goodbye. He walked across the small yard to the sidewalk and headed in the direction of his house.

Nora stood behind the screen door sobbing behind trembling fists. She bit into the soft part of her thumb. She pressed her hand against the screen and a crimson splotch blossomed. "Hey Nate, what do you think?" she squeaked.

Chapter 25

Nate was far from gloating over the most courageous moment in his life, rather he felt like whatever power had led him to Nora's wanted him to rest now.

Outside the kitchen window, two sparrows argued for the best place on the birdfeeder that he had replenished the night before. Nate found coffee already made. He poured a cup and went out onto the redwood deck behind the house. There, he found Grandpa doing stretches that looked like something out of an old Army training film. The stiffness from the day before seemed to have disappeared.

The deck was the last project he and his dad had built together. He dropped into a chair at the patio table and gazed up into the Jacaranda tree that hung overhead.

"Morning, Grandpa." He took a sip of coffee. This was his favorite seat in the house. Every summer clusters of lilac-colored flowers shaped like trumpets bloomed by the hundreds.

Grandpa Jack straightened up from touching his toes.

"Out exercising?" He asked.

"Just went for a walk."

Grandpa paused in the middle of a toe-touching exercise. "Walking is good for you." He wore only his boxer shorts and a white t-shirt. "After we check on your boat this morning, I want to go by the high school to make sure that you can return to your classes tomorrow."

"I'm not ready to go back to Pier Pont," Nate said, still gazing up at the tree. Most of the flowers had fallen, but he spotted one remaining on a lower branch. He stood up on the patio chair and plucked it off. "Come on, let's go to the harbor."

Nate and Grandpa arrived at Ventura Harbor. They weaved their way through a maze of lobster traps on the Kuda dock. Nate spotted his dinghy tied up just where he'd left it. He looked out beyond the breakwater. "See that boat out there, the one with the blue sail cover?"

"That her?"

"Yep," Nate said proudly.

"Looks like a beauty. Let's fire up the outboard and get over there," said Jack. He stepped into the bow of the small inflatable and nearly lost his balance.

Nate primed the engine by squeezing the pump in the gas line and then took a mighty pull on the starter handle. The little engine coughed and then sputtered to life. A plume of white smoke settled on the water behind the dinghy. Nate released the bowline and steered the dinghy towards the yacht basin where *No Worries* hung on her anchor.

"Hallo Nate!"

Nate recognized windswept Brian, the lonely-looking guy who had helped him and Nora anchor the boat in the yacht basin.

"You going to stop?" Grandpa asked.

"What for?"

"Well if he's standing on a dock, I'll bet he knows more about sailing than me. You're going to need some help."

Nate reluctantly guided the dinghy over to the dock. The guy had shown him up in front of Nora.

"What's up?"

"Just hanging out." Brian stuffed his hands in his jeans pockets and kicked at a rusty cleat.

"You still at Pier Pont?"

"I guess." Brian took the bowline from Grandpa Jack and lassoed the cleat, snugging the dinghy against the dock.

"I'm Jack." Grandpa Jack extended his hand and Brian caught it in a soul shake.

"You going out to look at Nate's boat?"

"Yep, you want to come along?"

"Sure, if it's okay with Nate."

Brian and Grandpa Jack looked at Nate.

Nate nodded. "Let's go."

He'd only seen the boat once in the daylight, the day of his dad's funeral. She was beautiful. Starting at the waterline, the sailboat was sleek. *No Worries* tapered forward from the stern to a stainless steel bow pulpit. Nate imagined Nora there, leaning out over the water watching dolphins dance in the wake.

"I can't wait to sail her to the island," Nate said.

Grandpa did his best to tie off the dinghy to the stern of the sailboat, but made a tangled mess with the bowline. "Don't you need to have some sailing experience before you go out there?"

"I learned some from my dad," Nate said.

Brian smiled.

"And this boat is paid for?" Jack looked amazed.

"Yep, Dad bought it just before he died. Rob, the guy who sold it to him, called me at the house the week of the funeral and told me the boat was mine," Nate said.

Brian held the dinghy steady. Jack climbed up to Nate who was already standing on the swim step. He lowered his voice. "So this is the place where you and Nora spent the night together?"

"Yeah," Nate said. He eyed Brian and repeated. "This is where we spent the night."

After rigging the mainsail, Nate was ready to hoist the anchor.

"You ready, skipper?" Jack called out from behind the wheel. The engine thumped steadily. Brian stood by at the mast, ready to hoist the main.

Nate nodded and started the electric windlass and the anchor lifted slowly off the bottom while the chain cranked around the turning drum, dropping into the chain locker. Once the anchor was secure, Nate gave the signal for Grandpa to put the engine in gear and head out from the safety of the breakwater. Brian raised the sail while Grandpa pointed the boat towards the big island of Santa Cruz.

He steered the boat for the harbor entrance and slowed as he neared a large red buoy, which marked the channel leading away from the harbor. The buoy towered ten feet above the water, while the flotation chamber at the water level resembled a giant red soup can.

Jack pointed to the sea lions that lay atop the can. "I've never seen so many in one place."

The sea lions' large bag-like shapes draped lazily over the buoy, warming their four-hundred-pound bodies in the early winter sun. Those that weren't lucky enough to have a spot on the buoy barked deeply, waiting for their turn to get on. The buoy rocked and clanged each time a swell rolled under it. A low horn atop the buoy droned every few seconds.

No Worries picked up the breeze and heeled to starboard. Grandpa Jack pulled the kill switch to the engine and all was silent except for the sound of water rushing along the hull.

After two hours of sailing within view of the coast, Nate was ready to head into the harbor and find a slip. He went to the mast while Brian fired up the diesel engine on their approach back to the harbor.

Nate loosened the mainsail halyard from around its cleat on the mast, but nothing happened.

"Got to let out the mainsail sheet," Brian shouted. When he released the line that held the mainsail taut against the wind, the sail flogged violently.

The mainsail tumbled down in a heap atop the boom. The long aluminum spar swung wildly. It hit Nate broadside and pitched him headlong into the cold ocean.

Sea lions swimming nearby disappeared.

Brian stripped a seat cushion from the cockpit bench and threw it to where Nate had disappeared below the surface.

Nate reappeared choking seawater. Although his flip-flops had come off, his jeans and t-shirt made it difficult to swim. He gagged from the scummy-tasting water. The air at the surface was blanketed in diesel fumes.

Sea lions on the buoy bellowed at the commotion.

Brian circled the sailboat around and Grandpa Jack hung his arm from the stern, but Nate didn't see it. He was distracted by the turbulence at his feet. He felt a strange sensation like something huge passing beneath him. Before he could think of what to do next, someone grabbed him by the back of the shirt so that it pulled tight around his neck, further choking him. He reached up and held on to his t-shirt so that it wouldn't slip over his head.

Brian had expertly maneuvered the stern of *No Worries* to within inches of Nate without running over him.

"Got him!" With one Herculean effort, Jack pulled Nate up onto the swim step.

The sea lions seemed to roar in approval just as the shark surfaced between the red buoy and the sailboat. With its gaping maw raking the surface, the shark caught a stray flip-flop in its teeth and gnawed furiously.

"Nate, get your legs up!" Brian spun the stern of the sailboat away from the shark.

Maybe it was the loud engine noise, or maybe the shark just lost interest, but suddenly the commotion was over. The only turbulence was from the engine.

"That was close," Nate said calmly. Strangely, he wasn't afraid, or even that angry at Brian. The moment when death seemed imminent, a sense of peace came over him. He reached for the chains around his neck and rubbed the St. Christopher medallion and the small cross between his fingers. First, the confrontation with Hans and now this. Someone was trying to tell him something.

Chapter 26

Sunday morning was now indistinguishable from the rest of the week. It used to be Nora's favorite day, but now it was just another waking moment of being chained to her dad. Nora awoke at seven and made her way downstairs for breakfast. Since the incident with Nate two days ago, she had nothing to say to her dad.

Nora went to the cupboard to get a box of cereal. While she was still in her nightshirt, her dad was already dressed in his Sunday sermon clothes, which consisted of a Hawaiian shirt, khaki slacks and a pair of leather sandals.

"How'd you sleep?" Her dad looked over the top the Sunday *Times*. He wore bifocals so his gaze was tilted forward with his chin almost touching his chest.

"Same as always, the sleeping pill pretty much knocks me out." In truth, Nora hadn't taken her meds for two weeks.

"Your medication is on the table." He'd placed the Melieron tablet next to a glass of orange juice on the small kitchen table like he normally did.

Nora popped the rose-colored tablet into her mouth and swigged down the juice. Her tongue maneuvered the pill to the side of her mouth between her cheek and gum. His eyes never left her as she pretended to swallow it.

"I'm going to get dressed for church now." Nora jumped up and went to her bedroom before he could say anything. She shut the door and spit the partially dissolved pill into her palm. She wadded the pill in a tissue and threw it into the wastebasket.

After church that afternoon, Nora and her dad stopped off for a bite to eat. Besides praying with her dad, eating with him was the only other way to find out what was on his mind. A waiter brought the drinks while they waited for their food.

"Dad, Dr. Asher thinks I'm doing better. Think I can start school next week?"

"I spoke with him yesterday and he thinks you're improving, but I want you to stay on home-study until second semester."

"Dad, that's not until February!" Nora couldn't believe what she was hearing. She was going to be trapped with him for another two and a half months.

"Nora, until the lying stops, you're not going anywhere."

"Who's lying?" She looked up from her soda, hoping she looked surprised.

"You've been up at night, sometimes for hours. I've heard you in the garage. What are you doing out there?"

She was busted. He wouldn't say anything if he didn't already know what she'd been doing. "Dad, I was just looking through Mom's old things. You know the ones."

For a split second, he looked like she'd just taken her knife and driven it into his heart.

Finally, the food came.

"Let's pray." He reached across the table to take her hands and she pulled away.

"What about you?" Nora shouted. "Mr. Holy Roller!"

He bowed his head and prayed without her.

"Flash! Pastor of the Surfers Church beats up sixteen-year-old boy in front yard!" Nora hissed. "I hate you!"

She slammed her fists on the table.

He chewed his food slowly, ignoring her. A dark calm reclaimed the territory of his face like an incoming storm. "This is between you and God."

Nora pushed her food aside and stared blankly out the window. The people that passed by the restaurant looked happy. Their relationship with God must be just peachy.

Silence ruled the drive home. Her dad had dropped another guilt bomb on her and then sat back while it destroyed any hope of getting her life back to normal. She would have opened the car door and jumped to the pavement if she could have, but he had control of the automatic locks. His silence was an indictment and meant to reinforce the guilt that blanketed her. She wanted to escape from him and die. She felt the familiar black fog that had temporarily cleared over the past couple of weeks close in around her.

A scratchy voice, barely audible, whispered inside her head, *"Cut me, just cut."* Nora's right index finger went to the side of her face opposite her dad. She clawed with her fingernail until she felt slippery blood rise in the welt. She touched the tip of her finger to her mouth; the coppery taste made her cry.

They arrived at home at a bit past two in the afternoon. Nora dragged herself into her bedroom and closed the door. She collapsed on her bed and wished for a knife. She realized that sleep was a temporary alternative, but without her medication there was no way that was going to happen.

Nora rose from her bed and went into the living room where her dad was watching a football game. She sat on the couch next to him and looked at his face knowing how much she resembled him; at least that's what people told her. How could she look so much like her father and be such a completely different person? She supposed that it was just another cruel joke that God had played on her.

"Dad?" she finally said. "Would it be okay for me to take another dose of my medicine?"

"Didn't I already give you your pill this morning?" He muted the TV and turned his attention to her.

"Yeah," Nora said, never raising her eyes.

"And did you swallow it?"

"Yes," Nora lied, "but I'm feeling extra sad for what I said at the restaurant."

He believed her, or at least she thought he did.

"I can't give you another dose of Melieron, but maybe the sleeping medication will help." He got up from the couch and went into his bedroom.

He returned and dropped a sleeping pill into her hand. "Here," he said.

She stared at it. The little white pill would give her relief, however short-lived. Nora went into the kitchen and poured herself a glass of water from the water dispenser. She placed the pill on her tongue and washed it down.

"Thanks, I'm going to lay down now," Nora said, standing in the doorway to the kitchen.

"Get some rest." He put the back of his hand to her forehead. "No fever," he said. His touch indicated their rift was over.

Nora walked into her room and tossed herself on her bed with the last burst of energy that she would have for a while. There on the dresser was a photograph of her mother holding her as a baby. She had pulled this from one of the boxes, forgetting to put it away a couple of nights ago. The photo of her mother was too beautiful and didn't belong in a cardboard box. No, if her dad saw it, he'd just have to deal with it.

She lay back on her pillow with her hands behind her head. It felt good to detest him. It was usually the other way around; she hated herself and tried to feel good about him. The sleeping medication was slow to take effect. The hatred that she felt for her father mellowed to an annoyance and she managed to drift off to sleep for a while.

***

Nora woke in the late afternoon. She was still groggy from the sleeping pill's deadening effect. She wanted to just turn over and continue sleeping, but forced herself to the edge of the bed and stood, swaying like a willow branch. Nora dragged herself into the bathroom and washed her face with cold water. The welt where she had scratched herself earlier had scabbed over. Her eyes were puffy like she'd been stung by a bee. But I'm still alive, she thought, looking at herself in the mirror.

Nora wandered into the living room, looking for her dad. He wasn't there. She opened the blinds enough to see their driveway. His van was gone. She went to the telephone, the place where they used to leave each other messages, and found a note. She picked up the small piece of white paper and in his neat printing, he wrote: *"Had to go back to church for a meeting, call my cell phone if you need me. Love, Dad"*

Nora didn't want to read into the note, but she thought he was communicating that he wanted to move forward. It was the first time he'd left her alone in weeks. Maybe, her finding the boxes was just a blip on his radar screen, nothing to worry about. The thought made her feel better.

She knew she needed to eat if she wanted the effects of the medication to mellow. Nora went to the pantry and peered in. She pulled out a box of breakfast bars. The choice was chocolate chip or dried cherry. Easy choice, she grabbed two chocolate chip bars and put the box back in the pantry. She took a bottle of drinking water from the refrigerator and walked towards the garage.

Nora stopped at the door and doubled back to her bedroom. Inside the drawer of her nightstand was her mom's silver cross. Nora rolled the delicate chain between her fingers. She reached up and clasped it behind her neck. Jewelry was normally not part of her wardrobe, but the cross was so beautiful. With a little rubbing compound, the silver finish would stand out against the etchings that ran through the pieces made to look like two tiny branches tied together. She wasn't worried about what her dad might say when he recognized it. So far as Nora was concerned, her mom would have wanted her to have it.

She went back to the garage and pushed the button to the automatic door. Late afternoon sunlight streamed in. She ate the breakfast bar with one hand and stood on her tiptoes looking on the back shelf where her mom's boxes were stored. Suddenly she realized that she was looking at empty space. She squatted down to look through the lower shelves and discovered they were empty too. Nora set her water bottle on a shelf and slowly walked backwards towards the open garage door trying to get a wider look at the sides of the garage. There were the familiar things like tennis rackets, camping gear and her dad's tools, but the boxes containing her mom's things were definitely gone.

Nora's face darkened. Tears burned down her cheeks. Her dad didn't have a meeting at church; that was a lie. He had probably taken the boxes to the church and locked them up in some storage room. She would never see those precious few things again and the connection that she had made with her mom would be lost forever.

Blood pumped so hard through her temples it felt like her head would explode. Mouth dry, she reached for the water bottle on the empty shelf. She sucked down half the bottle in one gulp. She was losing control. She felt the black fog of depression reach her insides, turning her stomach and make her chest ache. Then hatred for her dad like she'd never felt gave way to incredible sadness and she had to steady herself against the side of the garage.

Vaguely, she remembered thinking she needed help. She stumbled into the house, leaving the garage door open. The roller coaster of hatred peaked before dropping her into absolute despair. She looked down to see her clenched fist crush what remained of the water bottle. She threw it against the kitchen wall. The anger seemed to focus her thoughts. Where were her meds? Where was the sacred Melieron?

She ran into her dad's room and rifled through his drawers throwing underwear, socks, and t-shirts to the ground. Her strength seemed multiplied. She could have easily pulled the head-high dresser over with one hand. She ran into his bathroom and threw open the door to his medicine cabinet. She looked for the familiar opaque brown container, but found only aspirin and vitamins. She went back into his bedroom and climbed onto a chair to search the top shelf of his closet. Two boxes similar to the cardboard boxes that had been in the garage were shoved in the back corner. One had a photo album on top of it. Nora pushed the boxes apart. There it was. She pulled the bottle of Melieron towards her. There was her name, Nora Nelson, and the instructions to "take one pill daily." Red warning labels flagged the container. Most prominent was the warning against taking the pills with alcohol.

"What the hell," Nora said. She popped two of the fifty-milligram tablets into her mouth. If there had been any alcohol in the house, she would have chugged it along with the pills, but her dad didn't drink. She pulled the large boxes and the photo album down from the shelf and hauled them into her bedroom. The least she could do to hurt him was to pilfer through his stuff.

Nora flipped open the photo album. Right away, she recognized the photos must have been taken in the hospital while her mom endured chemo treatments. She wore a different colored headscarf in all of the photos, except one when her hair was still intact and its natural sandy blond. Nora was five years old in the photos and each picture of her with her mom astounded her. She gasped, holding her hand to her mouth. Her mom, Sarah, had the most magnificent smile, however thin and pale, and still managed to beam despite the pain she must have felt from the breast cancer. Nora imagined that her mom was smiling because of her.

She sat on the floor looking at the photos for thirty minutes before realizing that her dad might come home any minute. Burning anger had given way to a melancholy drunkenness caused by the overdose of her meds. Her eyes clouded with tears. Nora was falling backwards into the vortex of memory.

"Mommy," she murmured as she turned page after page of the album. She came to the last photo. Her mom was surrounded by family. There were her grandparents, Sarah's mom and dad and her dad's parents, all looking much younger, but no Nora. She closed the photo album gently. She pulled open the box and inside she found clothes, but not street clothes. These were nightgowns. Soft velvety things and under them the headscarves that she'd seen in the photos.

These must have been the things her mom wore just before she died. Nora pulled the colored scarves from the bottom of the box and held them to her face, hoping to smell any scent that might remind her of her mother. Tears had dried and Nora's eyes were left red and swollen. She glanced in the bottom of the box and there was a book. No, it was a journal. She recognized her dad's neat handwriting. The dates began in the months prior to her mom's death. The journal entries seemed to match the photos. She flipped forward to a later date. She couldn't believe her eyes. *"Today I buried Sarah's ashes on Santa Cruz Island...."*

Nora shuffled through clean blank pages. Then a recent date. *"Nora is weak in spirit. She runs from her problems. I may never be able to tell her the truth about Sarah."*

"Me, weak?" she shrieked.

How dare he call her weak—*he* was the one avoiding things. Weak? She'd show him weak. She'd go to the island and find her mom's grave.

Nora teetered and nearly fell when she tried to stand up. She couldn't believe her Dad had buried her mom on the island and never told her. She'd always thought maybe her mom's ashes had been scattered at sea, but of course her dad never talked about it. Nora's anger flared again. All those times they'd surfed together and looked out at Santa Cruz Island, and he'd never told her that's where her own mother was buried!

Nora was sedated, that was for sure, but she knew that if she didn't get out of the house with the album and the journal her dad would take them from her just like he had everything else. She went into her room and put on her running shoes. She grabbed her jacket and her backpack from school. Nora emptied the useless textbooks onto the floor and stuffed the photo album and her father's journal inside.

She looked under her mattress for her own journal and discovered it was gone. That was the last straw. It was ironic they were reading each other's private thoughts, but she was still indignant. He shouldn't have taken it. Nora was determined to leave him now, forever.

She rifled through her drawers for the emergency credit card that her dad had given her last summer when they traveled to the east coast. Before she left, she found the envelope containing one hundred dollars in cash that she had earned babysitting at the church. She grabbed some extra clothes and shoved them all into the top of the pack. And suddenly, she remembered.

Nora jogged into her dad's bedroom and picked up the pill bottle from the floor. She jammed it into her pack before zipping it closed. Nora slung the bulging pack onto her shoulders and ran out the front door, not even bothering to close it behind her.

Chapter 27

At 3 p.m., Nate walked out of Pier Pont High School wondering if he'd ever see Nora again. It had been two days since the incident with Hans and as much as he wanted to call her, he didn't. He'd returned to Pier Pont like Grandpa Jack had asked and re-entered his classes.

Other than Nora's absence, nothing much had changed. The teachers and students in all of his classes welcomed him back. It amazed him that people who never talked to him before made a point of telling him how sorry they were that his dad had died.

Like a circadian rhythm that he'd lived by for years, Nate automatically trudged in the direction of his mom's house after school. Suddenly he realized that he was walking in the wrong direction. He no longer had to live with her. He switched direction and nearly ran all the way home—his real home.

"Grandpa, you home?" A news station played on the stereo in the living room.

"I'm out back." The sliding glass door was open to the backyard. Grandpa Jack was sitting at the patio table with a sheaf of papers spread over the glass tabletop.

"House looks good."

"I hired a gal. She came by this morning and gave it a scrubbing," Grandpa said.

Nate nodded. He liked the idea of having a maid. His dad had always divided the cleaning duties between them, yet nothing ever seemed to get done.

"We still going to the store?"

"Yes, but I have some news to tell you first."

News couldn't be good. He dropped his pack next to the table and sat down. In front of Grandpa Jack was a stack of old court documents. Nate's heart skipped a beat when he recognized his parents' divorce papers from years past.

"So you're probably wondering why I'm looking at these."

The old worn-out legal file was accordion-like and had an elastic tie in the front to hold it closed. Nate hadn't seen the file in at least eight years. He remembered seeing it a lot when he was in the first grade. His dad had kept his drawings and all of his completed schoolwork in a similar-looking one. One time he had an important meeting at the courthouse and took the wrong file, the one with Nate's first-grade work in it. After that, his dad wrote in big block letters "LEGAL" across the front of the file. He probably would have preferred to write "DIVORCE."

Seeing the file over the years served as a constant reminder of his parents' fight over him. It held a prominent position on the shelf next to the television. Whenever his dad had argued with his mom on the telephone about his custody arrangement, he would pull the file from the shelf and begin quoting from the divorce documents. Eventually, the file was put on the closet shelf next to his dad's old tax returns and forgotten.

"Mom called, didn't she," Nate said with certainty. All of the hopefulness of the past three days died.

"Yes, Tammy did call," Grandpa Jack said. He began organizing the papers so he could return them to the file. "She just wanted to see how you were doing. Said she'd called Idaho and was surprised you weren't there."

"And what did you tell her?" Nate asked.

"Told her you started school today and seemed to be settling back into your life here quite well." Grandpa Jack pushed his chair away from the table and looked up into the Jacaranda tree next to the deck. Both were silent as the small black birds chattered away in the treetop above. A cluster of lilac-colored flowers had fallen onto the legal papers that remained on the table. Grandpa picked up the flower and examined it before dropping it over the redwood deck onto the grass.

"Nate, Tammy wants to see you and wants you to spend tonight at her house," Grandpa Jack said.

"I knew it! We should have never come back here!"

Nate slammed his fist on the table, rattling the glass. His ears felt like they were on fire. Nate saw that his grandfather had more to say. "Come on Grandpa, spill it! Tell me everything!"

"When your mom called this morning..." Jack chose his words carefully. "She was upset that I didn't have you call her when we returned to Ventura." He paused, his voice softened. "She just wants to see you, Nate."

It was obvious that his grandfather was not going to tell him everything, but he could figure it out on his own. She was laying claim to her custodial rights, just like she had all those years after divorcing his dad.

"I'm not going back!" Nate booted his backpack across the deck.

"Nate, you have to. Tried negotiating with her, but she said she had the law on her side, whatever that means."

"I don't care about the stinking law. The law doesn't care if I'm held prisoner in her house for the next two years. She only wants me for the money. Since my dad's dead and not giving her money, I'll have to go to work to help her pay the bills!"

Grandpa Jack leaned against the frame of the sliding glass door like more weight had just been stacked on his shoulders. "You think money is the only reason?" He cleared his throat as if the words needed loosening. "Maybe she just misses you."

"Yeah right!"

She had constantly shared her financial woes with him, telling him if it hadn't been for the child support, she would have moved away from the beach a long time ago.

"Nate, when you're eighteen you can make your own decisions. But until then, you have to live with your mom if that's what she wants. She's your legal guardian."

Nate said nothing. He went into the living room and threw himself on the couch. Time was what he needed, but how could he stall her? Just when things were getting better, they got worse. A couple days of peace and stability and wham! Everything got turned upside down again. Then, he had an idea.

"Grandpa, come here," Nate said.

"What is it?"

"I'm not feeling well." Nate stretched his feet out on the couch. "When did she say she was coming to get me?"

"She told me she'd pick you up by five."

"If there's one thing she can't stand, it's taking care of me when I'm sick." Nate was almost joyous that he'd thought of this. "Not once that I can remember has my mom taken care of me when I've been sick. She's terrified of catching anything. When I was a kid, I wasn't allowed to return to her house until I was completely well."

"Go on," said Grandpa.

"I've never done this before, so you better watch out," Nate said. He got a small brown bottle from the bathroom. It was Ipecac, a medicine used to induce vomiting after a kid swallowed something that he wasn't supposed to. Probably every parent that raised children knew about it, except his mom. Two tablespoons of the stuff and a glass of water would have him puking in a few minutes.

"Take a look." Nate handed Grandpa Jack the bottle.

"That's very clever," Grandpa said, reading the label.

"In about five minutes, I'll take some and by the time she walks in here, I'll be puking plenty. You watch."

"Oh, I will," Grandpa said.

Right at five o'clock, there was a knock at the front door. Grandpa Jack peered out from behind the blinds. Nate had sucked down a couple tablespoons of the medicine a few minutes earlier and was starting to feel queasy.

"Nate, she's here. You ready?"

"Yeah." He didn't know if he could hold it in much longer.

"There's a black BMW at the curb with a guy at the wheel. Anybody you know?"

"Naw, probably a new boyfriend." If she didn't hurry up and come into the house, Nate was going to hurl too soon.

Jack opened the door. "Tammy," he said, forcing a smile.

"Where's Nate?" His mom looked past Grandpa Jack into the living room. She already sounded ticked off.

"He's right there." His grandpa moved aside so that she could see Nate lying on the couch.

"What's wrong with him?" His mom raised a hand to her chin.

"When he came home from school, he wasn't feeling well," Grandpa said.

"Hey Mom." Nate covered his eyes like he was shielding them from a glaring light. He hoped that he looked as crummy as he felt. He waved her closer. "Let me hug you." He reached out to her weakly.

His mom wore a pair of new heels with a sequined skirt and a matching blouse that plunged at the neck. The outfit was likely meant to impress her new friend in the BMW. She tiptoed to the couch like she was walking in mud. Just as she bent down to touch Nate's outstretched hand, he sat up and lurched towards her, grabbing the waste basket that he had set beside the couch. Nate gagged once before emitting a long spew of vomit into the basket. His mom covered her mouth, looking like she might throw up herself.

"Oh my god, what's wrong with him?"

Grandpa Jack ran into the kitchen. He returned to the living room with a bottle of water. His mom grabbed it and gulped half of it down.

"Thanks, Jack." She wiped the corner of her mouth with the back of her hand. She turned away when Nate dry heaved into the trashcan.

Grandpa Jack returned from the kitchen with yet another bottle of water and gave it to Nate. "I think the stress that he's been under lately has finally caught up with him."

"Thanks, Grandpa." Nate took a sip from the water bottle.

His mom backed up to the front door. "Nate honey, call me when you feel better, okay? Then I'll come for you and take you home." She scowled at Grandpa Jack on the way out.

"I'll take good care of him," Grandpa said. He followed her out the front door down to the driveway.

Nate jumped up from the couch to watch from behind the blinds. He put his ear close to the screen of the open window to hear their conversation. At first he thought the medication had kicked back in and he was about to be sick again. Then the jagged edge of a memory hit him between the eyes. When his parents had divorced, he would sit at this window and watch them fight. They'd argue every time his mom dropped him off. Sweat beaded on Nate's forehead as he pressed it to the screen. It sounded the same now as it had nine years ago.

"I can't believe you, Jack!" his mom said. "I allow Nate to stay with you a couple of weeks and you get him sick." Nate couldn't hear his grandfather's soft-spoken response.

Nate didn't recognize the guy in the BMW. If it wasn't her boyfriend, it was probably her lawyer.

"I'll call tomorrow to see how he's doing," Nate heard his mom say. She whirled around on her new heels and clacked down to the curb to the waiting car.

Nate was in the backyard rinsing out the wastebasket when Grandpa Jack came out onto the deck. He looked worn out.

"You should win an award for that puking performance," he said.

"What did I tell you? She doesn't want to have anything to do with me when I'm sick."

"Can't be sick forever. She's going to call again tomorrow. How many days you think you'll get out of this stunt?"

"Three, maybe four." Nate rinsed out his mouth with the garden hose before shutting it off.

"It's not going to work."

"Why not?"

"Because she's going to come over here and check up on you. She said she might even take you to the doctor. Then what?" Grandpa Jack went back in the house.

Nate set the trash can upside down to dry and followed him inside. "Have you told anyone about *No Worries*?"

"Only your grandma."

"That's it then. I'll hide out there until my mom stops looking for me."

"And I'll stay here and pretend I don't know what's going on? Forget it, I'm not helping you run away." He shook his head and looked out the patio window. "Should have stayed in Idaho."

"Don't worry, you're not involved."

"Too late for that." Grandpa Jack pulled a beer from the refrigerator and sat down at the kitchen table. He looked a lot like Nate's dad when he was worried about paying the mortgage on time. "Just remember one thing."

Nate took a Coke from the refrigerator and sat down next to Grandpa on the couch.

"When this thing with your mom gets ironed out, the truth usually lies somewhere in the middle."

"What do you mean?"

"Your mom may not be the person you've always expected her to be, but she loves you."

"Sure." Nate shucked off his t-shirt and went to his room to change.

They went out to buy groceries as planned. The only difference was they bought for two homes, rather than one. Nate would need provisions if he was going to live as a fugitive aboard the sailboat.

Chapter 28

Another bottle shattered against the grid works of the bridge above her. Nora curled tightly into the fetal position, trying to make herself invisible.

"I'm gonna kill you!" A woman's drunken scream punctuated the rumble of a truck overhead. Nearby, someone stumbled through the brush. The person stopped so close to Nora she could hear him belch and then urinate.

Nora had spent a sleepless night huddled in the dry riverbed near the harbor. A collection of homeless people terrified her every moment. When daylight came, she was afraid to come out for fear of being spotted. Hungry and afraid, Nora made a run for the harbor. She felt a manic episode coming on and the only thing that she could do was pop a couple of pills and hope for the best.

With her ponytail streaming a foot behind her, Nora sprinted towards the harbor like a runaway maverick. Nostrils flaring, she inhaled huge volumes of oxygen with every stride. The twenty-pound backpack did nothing to slow her. The two Melieron tablets that she had taken did little to curb the almost supernatural spike of energy that propelled her towards the marina. Her goal was to find the abandoned sailboat that she had seen a few weeks ago when they anchored *No Worries* in the yacht basin. Going to Nate's boat, even if it was still moored in the same place, was too risky. Her dad would call on Nate for sure when he figured out that she'd run away.

The maddening clang from the rigging of a hundred sailboats drove her sleepless mind into manic overdrive. Nora stopped at the foot of a dock and spun around trying to get her bearings. If she could just find Brian, he would know where to find the abandoned sailboat. Going back to the river bottom wasn't an option. She cupped her hands to her mouth. "BRIAN! WHERE ARE YOU?"

On the next dock, Nora saw a woman peering over the stern of a large cruising yacht. In the gray light she couldn't make out whether the woman heard her or not. "EXCUSE ME! YOU KNOW BRIAN?"

At first, the woman didn't reply, then she said, "If you wish to speak to me, you will have to come over here!"

Nora hitched her thumbs through the shoulder straps of her pack and jogged around the maze of docks until she recognized the large offshore cruising sailboat where Brian lived. The woman, probably Brian's mother, stood on deck with her arms crossed. She wore a yellow foul weather jacket while Nora stood there in a t-shirt.

"Did Brian know you were coming?"

"No. I'm a friend." She remembered him mentioning that he went to Pier Pont High. "I need to ask him about some homework."

"He's not here. He's gone to the store with his dad."

"I'll wait then." Nora took off her pack and nervously stepped off the gnarled boards on the dock. "One, two, three…" A bundle of nerves, she didn't know what else to do.

"You can come aboard if you'd like," the woman said. Her voice softened. "What's your name anyway?"

"Jane, what's yours?" Nora didn't intend to be rude. It just came out that way.

"My name's Susan. Jane, please come inside and wait. It's getting cold and it's going to be dark soon." She zipped up her yellow slicker against the chill.

Nora's mind ran wild. What if Brian's mom called the police? Worse, what if she knew her dad and called him?

"Thanks, I'll just wait here."

"If you change your mind, I'll be below." The woman looked as if she might say something more and then disappeared down the cavernous companionway stairs.

Nora took off her pack and sat cross-legged at the end of the dock. Fish stirred the calm surface of the water. Even if Brian came home, Nora doubted his mom would allow him to help her.

After waiting for twenty minutes, Nora rapped her knuckles against the sailboat. "Anybody in there?"

No one answered. This time she pounded her fist against the fiberglass hull.

Brian's mom returned to the deck with a portable telephone pressed to her ear. She covered the receiver with her hand. "Are you okay?"

"Just tell Brian I stopped by. My name's really Nora," she said.

Brian's mom had to be calling the police. She shouldn't have given her real name. Nora shouldered her pack and ran up the dock towards the gate. She needed to find the abandoned sailboat before nightfall.

After a frantic hour of searching every dock in the marina, Nora finally found the boat she was looking for. The marina had moved the derelict boat to the far end of a dock that looked like it was ready to sink. Even in the dark, the abandoned boat looked like a wreck. The topsides were covered with white guano from seagulls that roosted on her deck. The sail covers were tattered and the waterline was coated with algae so thick it looked as if the sailboat might be attached to the bottom.

Nora tried the doors that led below deck. They were unlocked and when she pulled them open, they nearly fell off their hinges. Feeling her way in the dark, she climbed down the steps and tossed her pack onto the floor. The boat smelled musty and damp. Worse, there was the faint odor of gasoline, which made Nora think that if she lit a match, the little boat might explode. Outside, a dock light cast a yellow glare that filtered in the cabin windows giving Nora just enough light to see as she rifled through the galley drawers. She found nothing but some old silverware and a bottle opener.

Scrounging under the navigation table, she found a single match. She was about to strike the blue-tipped match against the zipper of her jeans when she saw the electrical panel. The switches weren't labeled, so Nora impulsively started tripping them. Click, nothing. She clicked again and the running lights on the bow pulpit flickered on. Another switch turned on the deck lights.

After flicking a few more switches, Nora managed to turn on the cabin lights. She looked around. Not bad for an abandoned boat. The cushions were clean and the wood interior gleamed with several coats of varnish. Other than the smell, it seemed to be a good place to crash for the night. Better at least than spending another hideous night in the river bottom.

Nora settled into the corner of the bench seat on the starboard side of the cabin. She pulled out the photo album and journal that she had found in her dad's closet the previous afternoon.

She opened it to the first page. It was dated January 11th, 1992, five months before her mom died. Flipping forward, she found that the journal's last entry was August 8th, almost two months past the date of her mom's death on June 10th, 1992. Nora read the journal from the beginning. She devoured the contents like she was studying for a final exam. It read part medical chart, and part true confession.

"February 11th: I made Sarah laugh when I came in to her room this morning dressed like Abraham Lincoln. I had to perform at Nora's kindergarten class for Lincoln's birthday later in the day and..."

At the end of each day's journal entry there was a list of drugs that her mom was given to fight off the cancer and kill the awful pain. New drugs and new treatments usually got headlines in that day's entry.

"Praise God, today is the day the paclitaxel will beat the cancer! Relieve Sarah's pain, Lord. Give her your indescribable peace through the methadone and oxycodone."

Nora consumed the journal page by page, only stopping long enough to go up to the marina bathroom and clean up.

The journal entries jumped forward from week to week and month to month. Rarely did her dad write in the journal every day. Seasons changed from winter to spring.

"April 11th: Today we went to Solvang. Along the way, we found a field of wild flowers and Sarah made us wreathes to wear. Boy did we get some strange looks. 'The flower family,' is what Nora called us."

As Nora turned the pages, she read how her mom's condition deteriorated to the point that her dad had to move her to the hospital. The description of her drug treatments intensified and the results that followed dominated her dad's writing. Then Nora discovered something she hadn't expected. The date was June 1st, less than two weeks before her mom died. Her dad had pressed a handwritten note from her mom into the binding of the journal. The note didn't have a date, just words in her mom's artistic handwriting:

"Hans, Every day that you and Nora come to the hospital to visit me is a blessing. Your prayers and good spirits always lift me up. I know I'm going to die soon, but I don't want to die in the hospital. I want to die at home. Please take me home, Hans. I'm weak, but my mind is still strong and I want to spend my last days at home with you and Nora. I want Nora to remember me smiling in joy, not retching in agony. Please let Nora remember me without the pain, dear husband. Do this for me and always tell Nora that I loved her. You know I never wanted to leave either one of you, but God is calling me home.
Love, Sarah"

Nora read the journal to the end. Her mom had died on June 10th, right after Nora finished kindergarten. She was thirty-one years old. Yes, her dad had complied with her mom's wish to die at home. According to the journal, she had died in the bedroom of their condo where her dad now slept. For some reason, the last few pages of the journal contained no reference to the drugs that her mom was taking. Maybe her dad had given up hope.

Nora continued to read beyond the date of her mother's death. Her dad described the funeral gathering in Ventura and the ceremony that followed. Many of her mom's friends paddled out into the ocean at daybreak, the day after her funeral, to lay wreaths in the sea. But other than that, the journal entries following her mom's death were sketchy and her dad's thoughts became increasingly difficult to follow.

According to the journal, her mom had wanted to be cremated and have her ashes taken to Santa Cruz Island. Nora learned from the journal that Santa Cruz Island had been a magical place for her mom, because that was where she had fallen in love with her dad.

On the last page of the journal, her dad described the day in August when he went to the island onboard a friend's boat.
"August 8th

Sarah has been gone for almost two months. As I sailed to the island today aboard John's sailboat, I sensed Sarah's presence and was encouraged to do what I knew I must.

I buried Sarah's ashes on Santa Cruz Island atop Mount Sacred Heart above Lady's Anchorage. In college, Sarah had called this the most beautiful place she had ever seen. She told me once that from the top of that mountain she could see our rooftop in Ventura. The two boxes that I buried at the foot of the cross will put our spirits to rest forever. I look forward to the day when I can see her smile again in the glory of a new body. No more cancer and no more pain. May God have a plan in all of this. And may He forgive me for what I've done."

Nora closed the journal and wept. Her mom had died racked by the pain of the cancer. But why had he spelled out all of the medications in the journal up until her last week of her life? And, he said that he had buried two boxes at the "foot of the cross." Nora thought that one box must have contained her mom's ashes, but what was in the other? Nora imagined her father, still fresh in his grief, hiking to the top of a mountain named Sacred Heart. She envisioned him carrying a pack with the boxes to the top of the mountain where there was a cross.

Nora looked at the small digital watch on her wrist. It was two o'clock in the morning. Before she closed her eyes, she remembered to set the alarm for six-thirty.

***

"Hey, Brian." Nora walked up behind him with her pack slung over her shoulder. There were five other students milling about the corner of Harbor Boulevard and Marina Way waiting for the bus that would take them to Pier Pont High School.

"Nora, what are you doing here?" Brian looked surprised to see her. "My mom said you stopped by."

"Yeah, well I just needed to talk to you."

"Oh." Brian avoided her eyes. "You live around here?"

"Well not exactly. My dad still lives in town, but I'm..." Nora searched for the right lie. "I'm looking for a boat, so I can move out." She didn't want to get into the whole dilemma about running away from her dad.

She saw the yellow school bus chugging its way up Harbor Boulevard towards the bus stop.

"Brian, can you take me out to Santa Cruz?" Nora blurted.

Brian looked at his watch and then up at the bus coming their way. "Yeah, I suppose. My parents have a launch that's pretty fast. We could probably drive you out there sometime."

"No, I mean I want you to take me to the island, not your parents. And I need to go there soon."

"Oh, so when were you thinking?"

"This afternoon, if possible," Nora said.

Brian took a moment to answer. It was almost like he was considering his busy schedule, but Nora knew that he was probably a loner and didn't have much going on. "Can you hang out until Thursday? My folks are going to a boat show in San Diego and I'll be on my own," Brian said. "I guess that I can take you out to the island then."

"Cool, I'll see you Thursday morning. Where should we meet?"

"You want to meet at my boat?" Brian asked.

Nora could see that he was embarrassed saying this.

"Sounds good, I'll see you there Thursday morning." Then she added, "Thanks, you're a good friend."

Nora waited until Brian's bus pulled up to the curb. She waved to him as the other students stepped on. The diesel engine growled and the air brakes released as the bus slowly merged back into the traffic on Harbor Boulevard.

Nora walked back towards the marina. She knew the city bus stopped in front of the Ship's Chandlery. She had to stock up on some provisions.

Chapter 29

Nate rushed to set sail from the harbor. Grandpa Jack had called to warn him that his mom was looking for him and she was on a rampage. She'd barged into the house and seized the photos of *No Worries*. She knew he was hiding out at Ventura Harbor.

The diesel engine had warmed up and all that remained was to cast off the dock lines. Once out of the harbor, the GPS told him all he had to do was steer two hundred and ten degrees for twenty miles and he'd be sitting at Smuggler's Cove on the island.

With a mix of trepidation and excitement, Nate stepped onto the dock to release the lines. He'd never sailed alone before, but it was worth the risk because the last thing he was going to do was give up and go live with his mom. Nate figured if he could just disappear for a couple of weeks, maybe she'd forget about him and become preoccupied with another one of her boyfriends.

He heard a beeping noise coming from below deck. Maybe the GPS was malfunctioning. Then he realized the sound was coming from the cell phone that Grandpa Jack insisted he have.

Nate picked up the phone and saw "*Jack*" spelled across the tiny screen.

"Hello?"

"Hey, it's me. I've been at the bank. Thought you should have some cash in your pocket just in case you want to buy me dinner this week. Can I bring it by?"

"No, I'm good, thanks," Nate said. "Got to go."

"I'm not going to let you do this."

"It's not your call to tell me what to do." Nate clicked off the phone and tossed it onto the aft bunk.

"No phone, no worries," he mumbled to himself. The thing would be useless at sea anyway.

He leapt up the companionway steps just in time to see Grandpa Jack hobbling down the gangway. The old man had a sea bag slung from his shoulder.

Nate went behind the wheel and threw the diesel into gear. He shucked off the dock lines and the sailboat lurched away from the dock.

"YOU CAN'T DO THIS!" Grandpa yelled. He dumped the bag and ran towards the slip. He stopped short, almost tumbling into the water. Jack raked a hand through his closely cropped hair and pointed towards the sky. He shouted something again, but it was lost over the rumble of the engine.

Don't look back, Nate thought. Otherwise, he might just wimp-out and circle back to the dock.

He remembered his dad shaking his shaggy blond head that last day at The Point. "No way," Nate repeated his dad's last words. "A couple of more waves, *then* we'll paddle in."

He drove *No Worries* out of Ventura Harbor keeping the red entrance buoy to his left. Sea lions lay piled atop each other on the large red can. The buoy's horn droned, seeming to warn him against venturing into the open ocean.

With the halyard fastened to the main, Nate's hands shook as he looped a coil around a winch drum and hoisted the sail. The boat dropped into the rolling trough of a swell as the light breeze filled the sail. Returning to the wheel, he spotted the island on the horizon and set a course towards the southernmost point.

Nate blew out a burst of air. "How am I doing, Dad?"

He cut the engine and watched the knot meter drop. He unfastened the furling line and the oversized jib rolled off the forestay. After pulling hard on the portside side sheet, the jib snapped taut like a gigantic white wing, heeling the sailboat to port. Nate took another wrap around the winch drum and cranked the sail tight. On a rolling port tack, the sailboat sliced gently up one side of a swell and down into the trough accelerating to seven knots on the downhill side. Nate calculated his sailing time to the island would be about four hours.

After a couple hours, he crossed the shipping lanes where mammoth ships plied the waters off the California coast. Nate saw a lumbering freighter steaming down on him from the north. He decided to change course, pointing *No Worries* higher into the wind. The change in course slowed the sailboat to a crawl.

By Nate's calculation, he was supposed to cross the shipping lane well before sunset. He needed to maintain boat speed for that to happen.

The wind was cold and the spray from the bow wake had dampened everything. Nate tightened down the wheel lock so he could go below.

Stiffly, he made his way down the companionway stairs. The sailboat bucked through the swells at a miserable three knots. He returned wearing the heavy parka that he'd brought from Idaho. He had the navigational chart under his arm.

Nate had remembered to turn on the marine radio below deck. All mariners, including the big ships, monitored channel 16. Nate had turned the volume high enough that that he could hear the radio's squawk from the cockpit.

As soon as he got behind the wheel, the radio crackled to life. "*All mariners in the Santa Barbara Channel. This is U.S. Coast Guard, Long Beach. Be on the lookout for sailing vessel No Worries. That's sailing vessel No Worries. Please report any sightings to U.S. Coast Guard on channel sixteen. U.S. Coast Guard out.*"

"NO WAY!" Nate shouted into the wind. He slammed his fist against the fiberglass bulkhead.

Looking south, he saw another freighter steaming down the shipping lane from the opposite direction. The behemoth looked like a runaway bull. The sun had dipped below the island and *No Worries* wallowed in its shadow.

Nate opened the chart in his lap. He wiped away tears caused by the cold wind. He'd planned to sail to Smuggler's Cove and anchor. Now that the Coast Guard was looking for him, Smuggler's would be too obvious. Where could he anchor for the night? Nate scoured the map for an answer. There, he smudged the chart with a damp finger. Lady's Harbor appeared to cut deep into the island. Maybe a boat could anchor there without being noticed. He scrambled below to the navigation table and punched in the waypoints for Lady's into his GPS. He pushed the command to determine his current position. It read he was only five miles away.

Nate made his way up the companionway steps hanging on tight as the boat yawed from side to side. "Got to steer two-thirty!" he said to himself.

When he pointed the sailboat higher into the wind, the sails flogged violently and the boat wallowed to a complete stop. Nate instinctively reached for the starter switch to the diesel. He turned on the glow plug and counted aloud, "One, two, three." When he turned the key, the engine rumbled to life. He focused on the freighter coming straight for him. Smoke poured from its double-stack.

"Need to get out of the shipping lane!" Nate motored full-throttle directly into the path of the freighter. He glanced at the knot meter and saw six, then seven knots. He remembered that his top speed under power was eight knots. The throttle couldn't be pushed any further, but he tried anyway.

He desperately needed boat speed. *No Worries* was driving in a path perpendicular to the course of the freighter. Couldn't the gigantic ship see him? He looked up into the spreaders. Nate remembered suddenly that he'd forgotten to raise his radar detector before he left the dock. Ships couldn't detect sails on their radar, but they could see a sailboat if she was equipped with a small metal sphere that reflected their radar signal. Without it, he was invisible.

If he couldn't increase boat speed, he would be run down by the freighter and sent to the bottom. A word came to Nate's mind: motor sail! That was it! He'd heard Brian use the term.

"Got to fall off!"

Nate swung the wheel to port and the sailboat responded. She heeled over while the sails filled with wind. Nate looked down at the knot meter mounted on the wheel pedestal. Nine knots and climbing. Nate ground the winch until the foresail was taut. The muscles of his forearms felt like hot irons.

"Guess that's why they call it a sailboat!" Nate clung to the wheel and leaned into the wind, feeling like a skipper in a Winslow Homer painting.

No Worries raced for the high cliffs of Santa Cruz Island. Where had the freighter gone? He looked downwind to port and saw the freighter's huge stern steaming off into the distance. The wake behind the ship was foamy and straight, indicating that it never altered course and most likely never saw him.

It was a narrow escape, but Nate hadn't time to revel in his sailing tactics. The sun was down and the twilight faded by the second. He needed to adjust course back to Lady's Harbor. Darkness fell and he found the toggle switch for the running lights and the compass. He checked his heading on the GPS before making his way topside. It read less than a mile to the anchorage.

The breeze puffed feebly and the main sail flopped one way and then the other. The problem was no longer the wind, but the strong possibility of running into the island.

Nate looked down to the instrument panel. The knot meter was spinning along at just under five knots and the depth gauge was showing that the water beneath the boat was getting shallow at fifty feet. He leapt below to retrieve the high beam flashlight Rob left behind.

On deck, Nate shined the light in every direction. The beam reflected against the ocean's surface, which was covered in places by huge patches of brown kelp. He realized that finding the tiny anchorage on such a huge island as Santa Cruz was going to be impossible at night. The only thing that he could do was to wait until morning and that meant dropping his hook in unprotected water. If the wind came up in the middle of the night, the sailboat might drag anchor and be dashed against the rocks. Worse, an unsuspecting fishing boat might fail to see his anchor light and collide with him.

Seagulls squawked somewhere in the distance and the sailboat rolled slightly when a swell passed beneath it. After a few moments, Nate decided to lower the small inflatable secured by davits above the stern. He would drop anchor where he was, then drive the inflatable in close to shore to find Lady's Anchorage.

Nate lifted his nose to the night. It smelled like the hills behind his dad's house.

Nate worked on lowering the inflatable into the water when he heard the rumble of another boat. What if it was the Coast Guard? He ran below and doused the lights that illuminated *No Worries* against the dark sea.

He knew he couldn't drift for long.

All was quiet, except the gentle sloshing the sailboat made while rocking in the swell. Nate squinted into the darkness. He heard the low steady thump of a diesel engine getting closer. Then he saw it. A white-hulled fishing boat stacked high with lobster traps moved slowly up the island showing only its green starboard side running light. It passed between Nate's sailboat and the shore moving in a straight line.

Without warning, someone aboard the fishing boat fixed a spotlight on *No Worries* as it passed. The blinding light painted a swath over his hull and across the mainsail.

The fishing boat slowed almost to a stop as the spotlight examined him. After a few seconds, the boat switched off its light and continued on its way.

Nate felt violated. What was the boat's purpose of examining him without saying a word? He listened carefully for his VHF radio to come to life, thinking maybe the fisherman would hail him on channel sixteen. He heard the occasional crackle and knew the radio was working, but not a word transmitted from the passing boat. Nate looked down at his watch, which illuminated 8:15 p.m. He was hungry and cold and he needed to make a decision.

He restarted the diesel and pushed the gear lever forward. He could barely see the single white running light on the fishing boat's stern. He jammed down on the throttle until he was driving in the fishing boat's wake. In a few minutes of tailing the boat, Nate watched it make a hard left towards the island. He followed the boat into a narrow passage that opened up into a protected cove. In the moonlight, he could make out the shapes of gigantic wash rocks that bordered the anchorage. The fishing boat circled around and faced *No Worries*. Was this Lady's? Nate had no idea of knowing. His GPS told him the anchorage was behind them.

The fishing boat backed its stern a few yards from the cove's sandy beach and then turned off its engine. Nate heard an anchor chain clattering against the steel hull of the boat.

Copying the fisherman, Nate circled *No Worries* until her stern faced the beach. He ran forward and released the bow anchor. The anchor struck bottom in twenty feet of water. The anchorage was silent except for the sound of the surge running up onto the sandy beach at the head of the cove. The slight breeze coming off the island straightened *No Worries* against her anchor line.

Nate didn't know if the other boat was skippered by a fisherman or a mass murderer, but he would be sharing the anchorage with him. He furled his mainsail and killed the engine.

Below deck, Nate kicked off his damp clothes, too tired to eat. He doused the cabin lights and climbed into the v-berth of the master cabin. He pulled the comforter over him and felt the bristles on his chin scratch against the soft material. Only a man could have sailed to the island alone, he thought. He was living his dad's dream and there was nothing his mom could do about it.

Chapter 30

Dawn lit the hilltops above the quiet anchorage, first pearl gray and then golden brown, while Devil's Peak was still shrouded in mist. Just outside the anchorage, a female great white shark swam lazy circles beneath a family of California sea lions. A young sea lion hunting for its breakfast surfaced for air just long enough to expose its belly to the glassy depths. Twenty feet below, the white shark snapped to attention and tightened her circle. Seagulls bobbing within close range took flight, but the young sea lion didn't sense the danger. In an instant, the shark took aim and launched its one thousand pounds towards the surface like a guided missile.

***

The sound of waves pounding against the rocks in the anchorage awoke Nate. He looked out the pocket-sized cabin window. On the island, hills dotted with oak trees climbed from both sides of a canyon that led inland off the beach. Two fat sheep grazed halfway up one of the hills.

Nate recognized the briny smell of low tide. He was anchored so close to the beach that he could almost jump ashore. To starboard, he saw the fishing boat next to him. Rust had bled from the fishing boat's hull leaving orange-colored streaks that reminded Nate of tears. Nate must have dragged anchor during the night to be so close.

A burly man dressed in dirty yellow foul weather pants fastened by a single suspender squeezed between lobster traps stacked on the fishing boat's bow. The man cranked in his anchor chain and found it tangled with Nate's. *No Worries* pulled precariously close to the fishing boat with each turn on the windlass.

Nate climbed on deck in his boxer shorts.

"Hey!" Nate shouted over the guttural thumping of the fishing boat's diesel. The man didn't turn around. Maybe the guy was deaf. Nate cupped his hands to his mouth. "Skipper, ahoy!"

"Your sailboat?" the man asked in a thick accent. He pulled a marlin's spike from his pocket and opened the stainless steel blade.

"Yeah," Nate said.

The man coiled a loop of Nate's anchor line in one hand and raised the four-inch blade.

"Don't you cut my line!"

The man cackled and held the loop over, as if pretending to hang himself. He was older than Nate's dad, but seemed younger than Grandpa Jack. He wore a faded blue sweatshirt beneath the dingy yellow pants. Seagulls screamed above his freshly baited lobster traps.

Setting the blade aside, the man barked a warning to the gulls in a foreign tongue so harsh it made Nate jump.

The grungy fisherman stepped inside his boat's pilothouse and returned with a short-barreled shotgun.

Nate took cover down the companionway.

The fisherman aimed just above his transom and squeezed off three rapid shots. Bird guts and feathers drifted to the sea behind his boat. He shook his fist at the retreating gulls. "Flying rats! Come back and I get you too!" He shouldered the gun and directed his attention, once more, to the tangled anchor lines.

He pointed at Nate. All but the index finger and thumb were missing. "You make me lose money, sailor boy! I have traps to set!" He dropped the shotgun on top of a lobster trap and took up his knife. Jagged words spewed like hot shrapnel as he tried to make sense of which line was Nate's.

Nate dropped below deck and threw on jeans and a t-shirt. He jumped into his dinghy and pulled the starter cord. He raced around to the bow of the fishing boat. By the time he got there, the fisherman had cut free his anchor.

"I could have untangled that myself!" Nate yelled.

"My name Lobster Bob. Ask for me at the dock in Ventura. I splice your line and teach you how to anchor at the island. All for free." He laughed.

Lobster Bob tied off the line leading to *No Worries* to a rusty cleat. He pulled a shackle from a milk crate on deck and quickly attached it to Nate's anchor line. After reattaching the two ends, he dropped them into the sea.

"Good luck sailor boy!" Lobster Bob said. "You leave my traps alone or I get you!"

Nate hit the gas and circled the anchorage. Colored buoys, the same as the ones on Bob's fishing boat, marked his lobster traps on the bottom. When he returned to the stern of *No Worries*, the two boats had drifted apart. He turned to see Bob waving his fingerless hand in his direction. The morning sun shone directly in Nate's eyes. It looked as if Bob was waving a handgun.

Chapter 31

Nora climbed down the companionway steps of the abandoned sailboat carrying a new backpack filled with gear. She had shopped in Oxnard for most of the day, buying things she thought she'd need to camp on Santa Cruz Island.

She spilled a grocery bag filled with snacks onto the boat's small wooden table.

"This'll last me for a while." Nora laughed like a kid on Christmas morning. She'd bought a sleeping bag and unstrapped it from the bottom of the pack frame. She yanked the goose down bag from its stuff sack and draped it over the bench where she figured she'd sleep one more night. After she had inventoried her remaining gear, she sat down to study a topographical map of Santa Cruz Island that she had purchased that afternoon. If she could find Mount Sacred Heart, the mission to find her mom's ashes would be that much easier.

Nora studied her dad's journal and reread the passage about how he'd climbed Mount Sacred Heart with her mom's ashes. It said he went ashore at an anchorage called Lady's. Nora ran her finger along the coastline of her map and read the names of the few named anchorages. She saw Prisoner's and Fry's, Platt's and Chinese, but no Lady's. And no Mount Sacred Heart either. It didn't make sense that her dad would get the names of two such important places wrong. Not a problem, she thought. She had enough food to last her a week and plenty of time to find the mountain.

Nora switched off the cabin lights and left the sailboat to see if she could get into the marina bathrooms to take a shower. They were accessible only by having a dock key, which she didn't have, so she'd have to find a way to sneak in. It was dark, so there was less chance of being noticed walking around the marina. Her dad had friends at the harbor; she was sure of that, so she couldn't let her guard down for a minute. Nora pulled the tags off a black knit cap and put it on, tucking her long blond hair underneath. She zipped her jacket past her chin and rolled up her shower things in a towel.

The gate at the top of the dock was unlocked, so at least she didn't have to climb over it. As she came up the gangway, she spotted Brian. He sat alone on a bench in front of the laundry room.

"Brian."

He looked embarrassed to see her.

"Doing laundry?"

"Naw, just sitting here," he mumbled. On land, Brian seemed to have lost the grace that she'd remembered when he helped Nate move his sailboat to the yacht basin.

"We still on for tomorrow?" Nora asked.

"My mom said that she saw you hanging around that derelict sailboat chained to 'C' dock. Says I have to come with them to the boat show on Thursday." Brian stared down at his worn out boating shoes. His blue jeans looked faded white under the florescent lights. His jacket was bleached many shades lighter from its original red.

Nora reached for the small cross around her neck and whispered a prayer, "Please."

She looked down at Brian, gangly elbows braced on knobby knees. He rested his chin in his hands. A shock of tangled hair hung over one eye. So artfully skilled at sailing, yet here on the dry he looked beaten down and useless.

"Brian, can you help me find a pair of bolt cutters?"

He looked up at her and shook his head as if he could read her mind. "Nora, you don't want to do that. Even if you're able to cut the chain, that old boat's in no condition to sail to the island."

"I'll just have to figure that out for myself. The bolt cutters, where I can get them?" Nora laughed at herself without cracking a smile, thinking she must have sounded like an outlaw.

"The marina keeps their tools in a maintenance shed behind the bathrooms," Brian said. "You'll need some help getting in there."

"Yeah, that would be nice." She hid her towel near the bathroom door.

"Come on," he said.

Nora followed Brian behind the bathrooms. There was an eight-foot chain link fence that surrounded a maintenance yard and a small building. Climbing the fence looked easy enough, except for the barbed wire at the top. Nora started climbing anyway.

"Nora, not that way! Come here." He led her around to the side yard away from the parking lot. He came to a section of chain link fence that was pulled away from the ground. Brian grasped the bottom and lifted until there was just enough room for Nora to crawl underneath. She squeezed under the fence on her belly.

"Okay, now what do I do?"

"The bolt cutters are inside the building, but don't turn on the lights, because the security guard will see them." Brian peered over his shoulder towards the parking lot.

Crouching low, like she had seen in the movies, Nora ran across the maintenance yard to the small wooden building with two large oil drums in front of it. "Lord, forgive me for what I'm about to do," she whispered.

She tried the door and found it was unlocked. Inside, Nora discovered a worktable scattered with tools. Hanging on the wall behind the table, she found the bolt cutters. She pulled them down, almost dropping them. They must have weighed at least thirty pounds. On the way out the door, Nora picked up an empty gas container. She'd never stolen anything in her life and here she was burglarizing the marina.

There was a hand pump on top of each of the large drums outside the door. Nora turned the pump handle on top of the red barrel and gasoline squirted from the hose onto her hand. She quickly filled the container with gas and dragged the gas and the bolt cutters to the fence where Brian was waiting for her. She slid her stolen booty under the fence, and then followed on her belly.

Brian helped Nora to her feet. Spotting the gas can, he said, "Good idea. Who knows, maybe that old engine will even start."

"I'll come back for these later." Nora spotted a clump of oleander bushes that stood between the bathroom and the maintenance yard. She stashed the gas container and bolt cutters under the low branches so they couldn't be seen from the sidewalk.

She retrieved her rolled up towel and shower things from next to the women's bathroom. "Brian, I don't expect you to help me sail to the island, but if you think somehow you can give me a hand, I'll be leaving tonight."

"My parents are expecting me back," Brian said.

"What time they usually go to bed?" Nora asked.

"Ten, ten-thirty."

Nora spoke on intuition, thinking maybe Brian's predicament was similar to hers. "Brian, my dad controlled my life from the minute I got up in the morning until I fell asleep at night." She could feel the anger rising in her face. She didn't have time to explain her entire life to this kid. "All I can tell you is that now I'm free. I'm planning to leave the dock at midnight on that old sailboat and I hope you're there." She turned to open the women's bathroom.

"Here." Brian unlocked the door and held it open for her. "Not that it's any of my business, but why do you need to get to the island in such a hurry?"

"To find my mom's grave," Nora said. "Hope I see you later."

"I'll try," Brian said.

A smile broke across Nora's face and she moved towards his cheek. Catching herself, she thrust out her hand.

After an awkward moment, Brian stuck out his hand. When he squeezed hers, it hurt. He loosened his calloused grip.

"Sorry," he said. "It's just that my hands are dry. Guess living on a boat does that."

She looked down and found the door handle, not wanting to look him in the eyes. "Bye," she said and slipped into the marina bathroom.

The exhaust fan hummed overhead and Nora listened above the drone to make sure she was alone. Nora chose a shower near the rear of the bathroom and pulled the curtain closed.

The steady stream of hot water seemed to wash away the guilt accumulated from hijacking the abandoned sailboat. She felt like she was about to do something of enormous proportion and stealing the boat was simply a necessary evil. Kind of like a soldier having to kill in the heat of battle. She had no choice in the matter.

After she brushed out her hair, Nora rolled up her things in her towel and stuffed the bundle beneath the front of her jacket. She walked into the cool night and went quickly to where she'd hidden the bolt cutters and the container of gas.

Nora reached behind the oleander bushes and dragged the stolen things from their hiding place. It was a weeknight so the walkways around the docks were virtually empty, except for a few live-aboards who congregated in the laundry room. The night before, she'd noticed that the security guard spent most of the time in his car, so he shouldn't be a problem. She carried the gas container in one hand and the heavy bolt cutters in the other. She spotted a man coming up the gangway to the gate. Not having a key, she could either make a run for it or climb back over the gate when no one was around. Nora decided to run.

She shuffled down the gangway weighed down with the gas container in one hand and bolt cutters in the other. The man on the other side of the dock gate looked up as he fumbled for his key. He looked at her face and then his eyes dropped to the bulge under her jacket where she'd stuffed her shower things. He paused, opened the gate and held it open while she passed.

"Thanks," Nora said. With the towel stuffed under her jacket, she must have looked like a pregnant boat-jacker.

Nora climbed into the cockpit of the derelict sailboat and dropped the heavy load. She hauled the bolt cutters to the cabin top where the chain was wrapped around the foot of the mast. She felt a pang of guilt for everything she was stealing, but if grand theft was the price that she had to pay in order to finally be at peace with her mom's death, then she would steal.

Once she figured out how to use the bolt cutters, she fit a link of the chain into the cutter's jaws. She pressed down hard enough on the long handle that her feet left the deck. Nora's one hundred and ten pound frame bounced against the arm of the bolt cutters with little effect. She checked the chain link for any sign that it had been cut and there was barely a dent. She looked at her watch; it was already ten-thirty. Brian said he might be there by midnight. She hoped he wouldn't flake, because she didn't have a chance trying to set sail alone. Nora decided to wait for his help and went below deck.

She couldn't help but think that her dad could come walking down the dock at any moment looking to take her home. She felt the familiar cloud of depression creeping slowly in around her. Nora knew from experience that she either had to sleep, or take another Melieron tablet. As much as she didn't want to, she reached into her backpack for the pill bottle. The rose-colored tablets represented the control that her father had over her and the little control she had of her own life. She swore to herself that this would be the last time she took the meds.

Nora pulled a tablet from the container and popped it into her mouth where it quickly dissolved.

She took her father's journal from her backpack and settled onto the padded bench to reread the part about where he'd buried her mom. When the Melieron took effect, she laid the journal flat against her chest and closed her eyes. The black fog lifted in her mind enough that she envisioned her mom looking down from Mount Sacred Heart. Before she fell asleep, she heard her mom's voice saying, *"Come."*

Chapter 32

Nora startled at the sound of the mast groaning against wind-filled sails. The meds had knocked her out. She threw her sleeping bag off and jumped to her feet. The cabin floor shifted and she fell against the bulkhead. Nora pulled herself to a sitting position. The derelict boat was sailing itself.

Nora yanked too hard on a galley drawer and it flew across the cabin, its contents scattering. She found the serrated knife that she'd used to cut open packages the day before.

She pushed open the hatch cover with the knife leading the way. When she peered out, she saw Brian standing at the tiller. Then she remembered. He had come to help her.

She pulled her hair back and redid her ponytail. Brian must have cut the lock and sailed them out of the harbor towards the island. She rubbed her eyes and stretched her arms into the onrushing breeze. "Are we close?" Nora asked.

"No, maybe another hour to the front side of the island."

"How long did I sleep?" Nora asked, looking at her watch.

"Well, it's 3 a.m. and you've been asleep since we left the dock around midnight." Brian stood facing her with the tiller pinched between his knees. He blew warmth into his cupped hands as he kept a lookout beyond the bow. "You know we got lucky tonight because there's no fog. Take a look."

Nora turned and saw the mammoth outline of the mountains of Santa Cruz Island thrust above the dark sea. She'd only seen the island from the coast in Ventura, and had never realized its immensity.

"That's incredible!" Nora climbed the rest of the way out of the cabin and hugged herself to stay warm. "Brian, thanks again for doing this for me, I mean I really appreciate it."

"Sounded like you had a pretty good reason for wanting to get out here," Brian said. "Where did you say you wanted to anchor again?"

"At a place called Lady's, that's all I know. My map doesn't show it. My mom's ashes are supposed to be buried on Mount Sacred Heart."

Brian nodded. She couldn't tell if he believed her.

"Nora, why don't you take the tiller while I check my chart," he said.

The wind exhaled and the old sailboat heeled to leeward.

"Just a gust." Brian's hand worked the tiller like a maestro. He gently urged the boat back on course.

"You want me to drive?" She grabbed the helm just as a swell slapped the bow. Nora yarded hard to port

causing the boat to lurch sideways. She grabbed Brian's
arm so she wouldn't go overboard.

"Whoa now!" Brian pulled her back to the center
of the cockpit. He hooked the tiller with the toe of his
sailing shoe and managed to swing the boat to windward.

Sleep had done nothing to mellow the intensity of
her quest, but at least the fog of depression was gone. She
lifted her chin to the dark wind and yelled, "He'll never
catch me!"

"Who?" Brian asked.

"My dad!"

"I believe you, but maybe you ought to just focus
on sailing," he said.

"Sure, I've done this before." She took a deep
breath and centered herself in front of the tiller. She
wedged her bare feet against the sides of the boat.

"Come on, I'll show you what to do," Brian said.
He stepped to the side so there was room for her.

Nora moved close enough to Brian that her
shoulder nudged his chest each time the sailboat lifted
against a swell. She zipped her jacket and pulled the
collar up under her chin. The clouds cleared shortly to
reveal a quarter moon. In the moonlight, Nora could see
that Brian was staring at her. She caught the wisps of hair
that blew across her face and curled them behind one ear.
When he tried to catch her gaze, she quickly averted her
eyes towards the bow, as if she was on the lookout. She
didn't want to give this guy the wrong idea.

"Okay Nora, you can take the tiller now, but just
take it easy." The darkness couldn't hide his nervousness.

Nora followed his lead. His sense for the wind was
beyond her. "Is this okay?"

"Perfect." He covered her hand with his. She wished that she'd brought along some gloves.

"I'm going below to get my chart. Just keep the boat on this heading. You see that mountain peak? Maybe it's the one you're looking for."

Nora could see the prominent shadow of a peak that rose above the ridgeline.

"Just steer for the mountain. Lady's should be somewhere below it." He waited a moment to see how she did on her own, and then leapt below deck.

Nora steadied herself with one hand and held the tiller in the other. She steered with a steady gaze upon the mountain.

Brian returned to deck with his chart of the island. He pulled two electronic devices from his daypack. One was a hand-held marine radio and the other a GPS device. It took the GPS no longer than a second to calculate the course and estimate their current boat speed.

"Nora, turn the boat up into the wind just a little." Brian stood looking at the compass that was mounted just to the port side of the cabin doors. "OK, hold it right…there, that's it."

The sails luffed slightly and Brian quickly trimmed them taut by cranking hard on the winch.

"Right about there should do it," he said. "We're heading two hundred and forty-five degrees at about four and a half knots. It's slow, but that should get us to Lady's in an hour. I don't know the name of that peak, but I hope it's the one you're looking for."

Keeping the little boat on course consumed Nora's attention. Then, when the wind lulled for a moment, she turned to Brian. With a goofy grin on his face, he sat on the starboard bench seat with his hands stuffed in jacket pockets. She sensed an opportunity to follow her calling.

"Brian, you think people go to heaven when they die?"

Brian's silly smile disappeared. "Don't know, never really thought about it before."

The wind puffed and the little boat caught a gust. Nora felt a wave of confidence wash over her, something she hadn't felt in a long time.

"Have you ever heard about the saving grace of Jesus Christ?"

Brian's looked down and shook his head. Then a grin emerged beneath his mop of hair. "What about that commandment?" he asked.

"Which one?"

"The one that says honor your mother *and* your father."

Nora wanted to drop it, but mumbled, "Yeah, that's right. The fifth commandment says honor your father and mother, so you can live a long life in the land God gives you."

She was a hypocrite and she knew it.

The wind howled in the spreaders and Nora gripped the tiller with both hands. She looked astern towards the mainland, expecting to see the familiar lights of Ventura. She slapped a hand over her mouth to cover her gasp. There was nothing there! Dark sky and black sea had become one.

Chapter 33

Nate had no sooner tied his dinghy to the stern of *No Worries* than he heard the crazy lobsterman's engine clang into gear and slowly motor away from the anchorage.

Nate ducked into the cabin. He rifled through a utility drawer until he found a knife. He unclasped it from its sheath and folded it open. If that crazy got close to him, he'd get him.

He put on a pot of coffee and scrambled six eggs in butter. Before he sat down to eat, he switched on the VHF radio and peered one last time out the companionway hatch. Lobster Bob had finally chugged around the point leaving only diesel exhaust in his wake. Squawking seagulls fought over the remains of the chum the lobsterman had pitched over his stern.

Freshly brewed coffee reminded Nate of the mornings at his grandparents' ranch. He'd call Grandpa Jack when he was ready, but not yet. He studied the nav chart while shoveling spoonfuls of eggs into his mouth.

He didn't want to take the chance of running into Lobster Bob again. He found another anchorage east of Lady's called Fry's. That's where he would go today. He fired up the diesel and went forward to hoist the anchor. He heaved the heavy chain hand over hand until the thirty-pound anchor was secured in the bow roller.

Nate made his way quickly aft to the wheel and carefully steered the boat out of the anchorage. He kept a vigilant watch for submerged rocks that could easily sheer off his propeller.

It wasn't long before the GPS beeped indicating that he was within a couple hundred yards of Fry's Anchorage. Nate swung his bow towards the cleft in the rocks that he thought must be the entrance. There were several boats already there. He couldn't take the chance of someone recognizing him. His only choice was to stay out of sight. That meant anchoring in remote places where others wouldn't risk spending the night. Strong winds howling against lee shores combined with poor holding ground was just asking for trouble, but Nate didn't have a choice. He continued sailing east along the front side of Santa Cruz looking for a place to drop his hook.

Nate felt a slight tremor of breeze. Going forward to the mast, he hoisted the main until the wind gave shape to the sail. He unfurled the jib, then turned off the diesel and heard the wonderful sound of nothing but the sea rushing along the hull. Nate's hands were sore from the line-handling that he'd done over the past twenty-four hours. But the pain gave Nate confidence that he was toughening into a real sailor.

In half an hour, Nate came upon Prisoner's Harbor. He recognized it from the pier indicated on his chart. There were several boats anchored there which, once again, compelled Nate to move on. If he didn't find a place to anchor soon, he would have to navigate the backside of the island. Using his binoculars, he followed the coastline past the pier and thought he saw something worth checking out.

He turned the bow towards the beach and in a few minutes, recognized the white foamy lines as the backsides of breaking waves. He carefully sailed within two hundred yards of the breakers. This was what Nate and his dad had dreamed of: surfing Santa Cruz Island without the crowds.

He looked at his chart and discovered the anchorage was named Chinese Harbor. It looked like the perfect hideout. Nate ran forward to drop anchor.

The noonday sun penetrated the aquamarine sea twenty-five feet down to the rocky bottom. Nate saw bulbous strands of brown kelp running from the surface downward to where the long graceful plant attached itself to the rocks below.

Silence mixed only with the sound of the breaking waves along the shoreline. Chinese Harbor was ringed by sandstone cliffs. At the foot of the cliffs was a deserted beach. Nate scanned the beach and cliffs for signs of life, but there wasn't a soul. He could have been a thousand miles from civilization by the looks of it. But he knew that directly across the channel, behind the low clouds and fog, was Southern California with its millions of people.

Nate managed to tug the resistant rubber wet suit over his skin. He hadn't surfed in weeks and either his wet suit had shrunk, or he was growing.

When he came up on deck, Nate saw the most beautiful wave curling towards the beach. He knew that his own surfboard was stored on the extra bunk next to the engine compartment, but this surf session would be in honor of his dad. He fetched his dad's longboard, which was secured to the portside lifeline. He unfastened the rubber gaskets around the board and checked that the wax hadn't melted in the sun. It was good to go. Nate attached the Velcro leash to his ankle and stepped over the lifeline until he balanced on the toe rail. The cool Pacific beckoned and he was steaming hot in the wet suit.

"This is for you, Dad." He threw the longboard into the water first, and then jumped in behind it. The cold ocean enveloped him and when Nate opened his eyes beneath the surface, he saw millions of white air bubbles stream above his head. He kicked to the surface and pulled himself up onto the board. Paddling the longboard through the kelp was easy and Nate crossed the two hundred yards to the breaking waves in a matter of minutes.

He'd never seen waves like this. The water was clear enough to see to the bottom. His only company was a curious harbor seal that looked a little like Nora's dad. Every few feet of paddling, the seal would silently appear in front of him and give him a serious stare. His glistening coat streaked gray towards his head. The seal must have heard the Coast Guard report.

Nate drifted over what he imagined was the take-off spot for the peak. He slid into the pocket of his first wave of seamless perfection. He rode toes on the nose and imagined his dad carving it up alongside him. He had never experienced such unbridled freedom. Nothing but the perfect wave, six to eight feet on the face with endless possibilities to turn and cut back. After each ride, there was a deep-water channel to paddle back to the peak and catch another. There was no rush to compete with other surfers. The surf break was all his and his alone. Nate painted a cutback and then brush-stroked moves off the lip until his legs ached.

No Worries bobbed in the swell two hundred yards to Nate's left. He checked her position from time to time to make sure she wasn't dragging anchor. He surfed for nearly two hours before he was ready to take a break. His arms had become rubbery from paddling non-stop.

After Nate had ridden his final wave, he began the long paddle back to the sailboat. He felt vulnerable paddling between the surf break and *No Worries*. The two hundred yards of open water all of a sudden felt dangerous. Nate's arms felt as if they were going to fall off. He was in good paddling condition, but he still had to take a break about halfway to the boat. He rested on top of the longboard in a thick patch of kelp thinking how cool his sailboat looked sitting at anchor.

Without warning, the water exploded around him. Nate and the longboard were pitched nearly upside down.

Beneath him, a gray blur rolled left, then right, caught in a death struggle. The wide-eyed harbor seal emerged from the bloody turbulence. In an absolute explosion of whitewater, a shark's snout drove the seal ten feet into the air. Wide-eyed and stunned, the seal splashed down within a few feet of Nate. Without hesitation, the shark came up again, this time leading with its mouth open. It took the seal in its maw and violently shook it from side to side. Nate watched in horror as the shark tore the harbor seal nearly in half. Blood and bits of skin with the blubber still attached flew. The shark's razor sharp teeth serrated the sea lion's flesh like paper.

As if given a signal, the seagulls that had been circling above settled noisily onto the kill site. They picked at scraps of flesh as the shark got down to the business of eating the mangled seal.

Shocked into action, Nate scratched for the sailboat, still two hundred feet away.

Adrenaline pumped new life into Nate's arms. The tide had swung low and large strands of brown kelp now lay across the surface making the paddle almost impossible. Nate closed the gap of open water between the kill site and the boat. He pulled himself along from one kelp paddy to the next, feeling like he was hauling himself across a great slippery brown rug. The surfboard's leash caught. Tubular kelp branches held him like tentacles. He was too afraid to stop and pull the leash off. There was no choice if he wanted to make it to the boat in one piece.

Nate stopped just long enough to lift his right leg behind him. In one movement, he ripped loose the Velcro strap. Free from the ankle leash, he continued clawing his way across the kelp-strewn surface until he reached the stern of *No Worries*.

"God, please save me!" He plowed the nose of the longboard into the stern of *No Worries* and in one lunge made it up onto the swim step. Once his feet were safely on the rungs above the waterline, he reached down and secured the surfboard's leash to a stanchion post. Nate's legs were rubbery. He hobbled onto the cabin top looking back towards the surf break. The surface in the anchorage was dead calm, yet seagulls still squawked near the place where the shark had attacked the harbor seal.

The tide had dropped dramatically since he first paddled out and the heavy kelp looked as if he could walk across it all the way to the beach. But where was the shark and all of the blood? Nate expected the gray monster to be circling *No Worries*, ready to devour him boat and all. However, the only movement that disrupted the stillness of the anchorage was that of a feral pig on the beach. With its bristly black hide, the pig waddled along the shoreline rooting in the rocks and sand with its short tusks. Nate thought how sad it would have been if he had died in the jaws of the shark with only the pig as witness.

He peeled off his wet suit while keeping a lookout on the cabin top. Not a boat in sight. The warm easterly breeze felt good on his wet skin. Nudged by a quiet whisper, something told him to get moving. But he ignored the premonition and stretched out on his back under the mast and closed his eyes. The midday sun warmed his bare skin. The shark attack settled into the back of his mind.

An hour passed and his curiosity got the best of him. He went below to get his cell phone.

He switched it on and listened for a signal. The cell phone flashed that he had several messages, probably from Grandpa Jack. He must have called while he was crossing the channel the night before. Nate tried to connect to his voice mail, but without any luck.

He couldn't use the VHF because the Coast Guard would be sure to pick up his radio signal and figure out where he was. He'd have to go ashore.

"If you're going to get me, shark, you'd better hurry." Nate gunned the outboard, lifting the bow upward like the wheelies he used to do on his bike as a kid. It took him a while to find a suitable place to land. The reef that he had surfed earlier was still churning out the waves. He landed on the far side of the crescent-shaped beach well away from the breaking waves. The bottom was rocky, so Nate killed the outboard and lifted the propeller out of the water before drifting in. He got out and waded through a cluster of partially submerged rocks, pulling the inflatable along behind him.

Once ashore, Nate dragged the dinghy over the rocks towards the high tide mark. He trudged among large clumps of kelp. Just to be safe, Nate tied the bowline off onto a fallen tree. He didn't plan on being on the island long enough for the tide to change, but he wasn't taking any chances.

So far as Nate could tell, this part of the island was deserted. He followed a trail that was wide enough that it could have once been a road. It led up a gully between the cliffs. Once Nate was high enough where he thought he could get a cell phone signal, he checked his message. It was from Grandpa Jack. He called.

"Hello?" The connection was hazy.

"Is that you, Nate?"

"Yeah."

"Where are you?"

"Can't say."

Silence.

"Hey Grandpa?"

"Can't hear you."

"Sorry."

Grandpa Jack cleared his throat. "Nate, I want you to come home. I've negotiated a deal with your mom."

"What kind of deal?" Nate gazed across the channel towards the mainland. His heart pounded in his ears.

"I've arranged a settlement."

"You bought her out?"

"Well, not exactly. You're mom needed the money-"

"Hey, gotta go! See you when I see you."

He snapped the cell phone shut. His dad told him once everyone had his price. He spit at the dry ground between his feet. That included his mom.

Nate followed the trail back down to the beach where he'd come ashore. He went to untie his dinghy and found that it had lost quite a bit of air. He searched the small boat and discovered that there wasn't a pump aboard. He pushed and lifted the dinghy until it was back in the water. It was as spongy as a deflated beach ball. Nate was surprised that he could even sit in it without sinking. He shoved off and when he thought he was in deep enough water, he started the engine. Nate tried to distribute his entire one hundred and fifty pounds across the floor of the inflatable. It looked like a hot dog bun and he was the hotdog. He gave the motor just enough gas so that seawater wouldn't flood in over the bow.

Faster, he thought, eyes glued to the stern of *No Worries.* Just get there.

He thought he saw a fin break the surface.

"Not again!" he screamed. "I'm not going down this way!"

The motor sputtered. Nate yanked on the starter cord. It came off in his hand. His weight shifted. Seawater poured in around him. The dinghy filled with water.

Twenty yards to safety. He abandoned the dinghy and swam. It turned turtle and disappeared, leaving a rainbow slick of gasoline on the surface. He sculled towards the sailboat. Kelp draped upon his shoulders.

Nate jammed his hand against the swim step. He levered himself into the boat. Drenched, heart pounding, he collapsed on the cockpit floor. When he could breathe again, he peered over the side. A commotion at the bow caught his attention. A 500-pound sea lion lolled on its side. The animal's flipper emerged perpendicular to the surface.

"You idiot! Thought you were a shark!" Nate pitched an empty soda can in its direction. It fell short. The sea lion disappeared and surfaced next to the can. It bellowed once and swam off.

With only his dad's longboard for shore transportation, Nate's island days were limited. He pulled off his wet clothes.

The sun had dropped behind the mountain ridge on the island. He dried off and returned to the deck. Reality set in that he could start living his life now. He could go home to Ventura without being on the run.

A cool breeze blew off the water. Nate ducked below and scrounged through his pack until he found the new sweatshirt that his mom had bought him. He pulled a dozen hidden pins from the new garment before shaking out the folds. He held it up to look at it. PIER PONT HIGH was stenciled across the front. He put the sweatshirt to his nose and breathed in the smell of newness. It reminded him of home.

New clothes were her way of saying she loved him.

"She is who she is." He pulled the sweatshirt over his head. "Guess I have to accept that."

Chapter 34

It would be light in another hour. The stolen sailboat limped into Lady's under the power of its sludge-choked motor. The wind had died and the ancient outboard strained to push the weight of the old fiberglass boat the last few miles to the island. Nora stood in the bow pulpit with the flashlight she'd purchased. She scanned the dark water looking for rocks. Her light swept across the hull of a commercial fishing boat at anchor. Brian circled the anchorage once before deciding to anchor in the northwest corner of the egg-shaped cove.

"Nora, can you steer?" Brian asked.

Nora took the tiller. "Where?"

"Just circle the cove once more. I'll get the anchor ready."

Nora steered the sailboat in a tight slow circle while Brian ran forward to the anchor locker.

After having circled the anchorage for the third time, Brian returned to the cockpit.

"All we have is a tiny anchor and about a hundred feet of clothesline. The best that I can do is put you ashore alone. I'll have to stay aboard just in case the anchor line breaks," Brain said.

"Good." The lack of sleep and no meds gave Nora's voice an edge.

"I'll get the anchor ready." He slapped the flogging mainsail.

"I didn't mean it that way." Nora had to shout to be heard over the sputtering motor. "Brian, I have to find my mom's grave myself."

"Sure you didn't mean it that way," Brian said, barely audible over the noise from the outboard.

When Brian dropped the anchor, Nora felt the sailboat lurch to a stop at the end of the anchor line. She was anxious to get ashore. She ducked below to get her pack.

Brian stuck his head down into the cabin. "Nora, we have another problem."

"What is it now?" Tempering her irritation was impossible. She had to get off the sailboat before she said something really stupid.

"There's no dinghy. How you going to get to shore?"

"I'll just swim in. Can't be that far," Nora said. She zipped up the top to her pack.

"What about your backpack?"

"If I can find a plastic bag, I'll wrap it up and swim it in."

Nora went through the boat until she found what she was looking for. "This should work." She found a trash bag filled with old clothes under the aft bunk. She emptied the musty things onto the cabin floor, and pulled the plastic bag over her pack. It wasn't quite big enough.

Brian went topside and returned with an old life ring encrusted in black mold.

"You can float your pack on this," he said.

"Perfect." Nora snatched it. "Now if you'll excuse me, I have to change."

When Nora heard Brian's footfalls on the cabin top, she changed into her bathing suit. She could hear the heavy surge punching against the rocks on the eastern side of the anchorage. The deck lights cast a dim glow on the dark water next to the sailboat. Looking out the cabin window, the surface of the sea was churned up, covered in a milky foam. Not a good sign. A storm was coming. She knew that much from all of her years surfing The Point. Nora hoisted her pack up the companionway steps and climbed up behind it.

"I'm ready." Nora supported herself against the open hatch. She wore a two-piece bathing suit. Her hair was pulled back into a tight bun on the back of her head making her look like an Olympic diver.

"I can pull the boat in closer to the beach if you want," Brian said.

"No, that's okay. I can swim from here. Man, it's cold!" Nora handed Brian her pack wrapped in the dirty black trash bag.

"When will you be back?" Brian asked.

"Hard to say. I'm staying until I find my mom's grave. Maybe you should sail back to Ventura. I mean, I don't want you to get in trouble." She hugged herself to keep from shivering in the predawn chill.

"No, I'll stay put. Besides, there's weather coming," Brian said. He looked towards the mainland, a pale light streaked crimson advanced on the eastern horizon.

"Yeah, I know, but I can't do anything about that. I've got to go." She nodded towards the dark island. She embraced Brian, hugging him tightly. "Thanks, friend." Before he could respond, she stepped over the lifeline and plunged into the darkness beside the sailboat. The beam of Brian's flashlight illuminated the foamy place where she had pierced the surface. When Nora came up, she blew out a watery blast of air. "Wish I had my wet suit!"

Brian handed Nora the life ring and she clung to it while he handed down her pack covered in the trash bag. Nora carefully balanced the pack on top of the life ring and when it looked stable enough, she began pushing the backpack towards the beach. Like a synchronized swimmer, she frog-kicked behind the floating backpack.

Brian shined the beam of his flashlight in front of Nora so she could navigate her way to the beach.

Halfway there, she turned and shouted in the direction of the sailboat. "Wait for me."

"I will, good luck," Brian shouted back.

Feeling like a bikini-clad commando, Nora made her way around the commercial fishing boat stacked high with lobster traps. After a couple of minutes, she waded up onto the beach. She waved an arm over her head signaling she was okay. The morning light was just starting to bring the surroundings into view and Nora could see the dark shadow of the mountain peak above the beach. She pulled jeans over her bathing suit and threw on a t-shirt. Nora shivered uncontrollably while trying to lace up her running shoes. She knew she'd warm up just as soon as she started hiking.

With her pack on, Nora disappeared into the trees that led into the hills. Beyond the hills was her mountain. The mountain that had to be Sacred Heart.

Chapter 35

High above Lady's anchorage, Nora believed she was climbing towards the summit of Sacred Heart. But a mousy voice, scratchy like a child's, kept a steady refrain of *"Wrong way!"* beating in her head. No chart named the mountain, but she was going to the top of this one anyway.

She hiked for almost an hour before stopping to get a water bottle from her pack. She'd been following a faint trail since leaving the beach. Nora unfolded her topo map of the island. It didn't show her much, except that the peak that she was hiking towards seemed to be the highest on the island at nearly 2,500 feet above sea level. She'd done little exercise since being locked up, so hiking straight uphill kept her drenched in sweat. She took a moment to rest against an ivy-covered rock.

Nora re-folded the map and slid it into the top pocket of her pack. She hoisted herself from the rock and resumed searching for traces of the overgrown trail. She pushed through the scrub until she found the narrow path, barely visible. It snaked its way up the steep hillside. As the trail steepened, loose dirt rolled beneath her feet like ball bearings. Nora attracted columns of tiny gnats that landed on her face and buzzed in her ears. She promised herself she wouldn't stop again for at least half an hour. She dedicated the next thirty-minute stretch to her mom. Under her breath, she kept a steady pace chanting, "Mom, this is for you, Mom, this is for you, Mom…"

After two hours of strenuous hiking, the trail disappeared again. Nora bushwhacked, kicking aside the scratchy undergrowth, until she came to a clearing on the side of the mountain. Far below, she saw the blue sailboat swinging on its anchor in the egg-shaped cove. From her vantage point, the boat looked like a toy in a bathtub. She knew Brian would wait for her and she felt guilty knowing she had used him to get to the island. Somehow, someday she'd make it up to him.

The straps of Nora's pack chafed raw against her shoulders, making each step a painful reminder of how much she wanted to find her mom's grave. She wanted to shed the heavy pack, but it contained the tattered photo album and her dad's journal whose words had motivated her to come to the island in the first place.

After three hours, most of it bushwhacking through thick stands of chaparral, Nora knew she was almost to the top. She could no longer see the sailboat, which was hidden in a fold of the mountain far below. Instead, she saw the whole Santa Barbara Channel stretched out before her. Looking out across the channel, she could see a large freighter steaming north towards San Francisco. Nora had climbed almost half a mile above Lady's Anchorage. Sweating profusely, she spread her arms above her head, as if in victory. A cool Pacific breeze swept upward from below, drying Nora's face and body. She shed her sweat-drenched t-shirt to her bathing suit top beneath. She slung the damp t-shirt over the top of her backpack to dry. It was mid-morning and she saw, at last, the sandstone summit, which she knew must be Sacred Heart.

Emerging from a thicket of chaparral, Nora dropped her pack at the base of the rocky summit. She ran her hand over a whale-sized boulder. The course surface reminded her of the popular rock climbing crags at Joshua Tree in the California desert. Last year, she'd camped there with her church youth group and had learned some basic rock climbing moves. It was time to apply them because the summit looked attainable only by following one of several vertical ravines that led to the top.

Nora removed a small daypack from her backpack. She put in her dad's journal, a camp shovel and a few supplies for when she reached the top. Great sooty clouds rolled towards the island from the west. If she didn't hurry she might be climbing in the rain.

Nora remembered her rock-climbing instructor at Joshua Tree telling her to always choose a route before climbing. She decided to follow the ravine that looked the least steep. Climbing hand over hand, Nora managed the first one hundred feet by jamming her hands into cracks that cut deep into the rock's rough surface. After a few minutes of climbing, she was exhausted. She wedged her feet into a large crack and leaned into the rock face, giving her hands a rest. The ravine became steeper the higher she went, but Nora moved deliberately upward, never looking down. The muscles in her forearms were on fire. She knew if she stopped again, her aching arms might fail her and she would fall.

Nora wedged her hands into progressively smaller cracks. Scraped raw, her fingers raked blindly at the rock above her for any hole or crevice that might support her weight. She twisted her feet into a narrow crack below her hands until both hands and both feet were committed to the same small fissure in the rock. She looked below her feet to see her new backpack being pilfered by a small herd of ground squirrels. No time to worry about the pack now, she had to keep moving.

Nora had climbed over two hundred vertical feet. Above her, the crack that she followed narrowed to a point where it completely disappeared. Without giving it much thought, she moved from the relative safety of the crack onto the exposed rock face. The tips of her fingers clung to tiny nubbins of rock that seemed sure to crumble at any second.

"Jesus, help me!" Nora squeaked from her parched throat. This was the end. She would die here.

A red-tailed hawk appeared in the corner of Nora's vision. She watched mesmerized. The hawk soared on an updraft.

Nora felt urged upward by an invisible hand. She found a fresh handhold. She pulled herself up enough to see that the rock face gave way to a steep, rock-strewn slope to the summit.

"Thank you, Lord."

Overconfident, Nora scrambled too fast and lost her footing.

Her left hand wrapped around an ancient pine. Stump and roots came loose. Dirt rained into her eyes. Blinded, she pushed her face against the rock. She slid, unable stop.

Through clenched teeth Nora shrieked, "Don't forsake me!"

The ball of one foot stopped against a protrusion. Nora launched her full weight upward, catching a handful of dead roots. She managed to sink the other hand into a loam-filled fissure. Hand over hand she clawed her way to the top. Finally, she was able to draw her knees beneath her and rest.

When she stopped trembling, she got to her feet. Nora circled the summit, about the size of the sailboat's deck. She shook her arms in an attempt to stop them from aching. The backs of both hands were gashed and bloody. Sweat ran down her wrists into the open wounds. Nora discovered the backside of the summit sloped gently into a dense stand of Torrey pine trees. She had risked her life climbing the steep face for nothing.

Nora had climbed to the top of several Sierra peaks with her youth group. It occurred to her that there might be a survey marker indicating the elevation and name of the peak. She found a boulder with a round metallic marker driven into its top. It read: Picacho Diablo, Santa Cruz Island, California. It listed the latitude and longitude, and gave the elevation of 2,434 feet above sea level.

Nora yanked her father's journal from the daypack and reread the passage. There was no mention of Picacho Diablo.

Could he possibly have goofed and buried her ashes on the wrong mountain? Nora laughed at the prospect, because her dad never made mistakes.

Sitting next to the survey marker, Nora pulled some peanuts and a water bottle from her daypack. She gazed across the high ridge of mountains wondering

which one was Sacred Heart. While she ate, gnats
swarmed on her scraped and bloodied hands. She fanned
the obnoxious insects away, and by mistake, knocked
over the quart of water that she'd carried to the top.

"Oh no!" Nora dropped to her knees trying to cap
the precious water bottle before it drained into the dirt.
Something metallic reflected in the sun. It was probably
just trash left behind by the last hikers to climb the
mountain. She kicked whatever it was with the toe of her
shoe and found it was solid. She yanked the folding
shovel from her daypack.

Like an archeologist, Nora scraped around the
metallic object with the blade of her camp shovel. She
pulled up a metal handle that was attached to something
buried beneath it.

Nora chiseled dirt away from the handle until she
struck metal below it. The possibility that this was
actually the box containing her mom's ashes was almost
too absurd to hope for. But a small voice whispered that
she had found what she was looking for, and not by
accident. After some serious scraping in the hard dirt, she
unearthed a heavy metal box about one foot square in
size. The latch on the front wasn't locked, but it was so
encrusted with dirt that it wouldn't open. Nora aimed the
shovel blade and with a powerful downward stroke, the
latch disintegrated upon impact.

Nora pried open the lid of the box and felt her
heart nearly jump from her chest. Inside the box was a
plastic bag. The bag cracked as she pulled open the top.
Nora lifted out a piece of folded paper that had yellowed
with age but was still legible. Underneath the note, Nora
saw a handgun.

She read the note aloud. *"I, Hans Nelson, willfully gave my wife, Sarah, lethal doses of morphine and other drugs until she died. I am completely responsible for her death. May God forgive me."*

Nora was stunned. Her dad had poisoned her mom with an overdose of pain medication. She remembered her mom's letter asking him to "Please make the pain go away," but she never imagined that he would poison her. Her dad had complied with her mom's request and evidently he was going to come back to the island and blow his head off. There was no other explanation for the gun. Tears streamed from Nora's eyes as she folded the note and placed it into the plastic bag next to the gun.

She took up her shovel and dug deeper into the hole, intending to rebury the metal box. Her shovel struck something metal again. She carved around another box of exactly the same shape and size. After a few minutes of digging, Nora unearthed a second box that lay buried below the first. She managed to pry open the lid and inside she found the dense gray ashes. A note lay on top of the ashes.

"August 8, 1992.

If you've found this box by mistake, please let it be. The box holds the remains of my dear wife, Sarah Nelson. We fell in love at this place: Picacho Diablo, Santa Cruz Island. We planned to return one day and renew our marriage vows at The Chapel of the Sacred Heart below the mountain at the main ranch. But Sarah died before we ever realized that dream. Please let her rest in peace."

Nora put the box down in front the small excavation site and gazed into the sky thick with gray clouds. "That's why he called this mountain Sacred Heart."

Her dad, always the pastor, probably couldn't bear knowing that the most memorable place in his life was named Devil's Peak.

The air had turned cold and Nora knew that she needed to get down the mountain before it stormed. Reason told her to return to the sailboat where Brian was waiting to take her home to Ventura. But Nora crossed her arms and straightened her back. She blew out a big breath like a runner before a race. No, she would finish the job. She would find the Chapel of the Sacred Heart and rebury her mom's ashes there.

Nora ran her finger through the fine ashes. Her index finger struck something solid. She pulled it to the surface and found a metal button, melted and misshapen from the cremation. Not sure what else she would find, she ran her fingers through the ashes again. This time, the tip of her right index finger found a ring. Nora scooped the ring to the side of the box. She blew ash from it. Studded with multiple diamonds, the ring looked unscathed. It had to be her mom's wedding band. Her dad must have put it in the box after the cremation. Otherwise, it would have melted.

A grin broke across Nora's face. She polished the ring against her jeans and slid it onto her finger. She admired the ring. "Dad, your plan wasn't meant to be."

Nora placed the handgun and the box containing her mom's ashes into her daypack. She folded her dad's notes and placed them between the pages in his journal. She buried the empty metal box that contained the gun and scattered rocks over the surface of the ground above it. Nora felt like she was leaving hallowed ground. This mountain known only by her mom and dad as Sacred Heart had kept her mother's remains safe for eleven years.

Nora walked off the summit through the grove of Torrey pines. She wound her way down through the pines, hoping to end up back where she had left her backpack. It was past noon and the darkening clouds blotted out the sun. A cold south wind stirred the dust at her feet. Nora had lived on the coast her entire life and she knew that a Pacific storm was on its way.

After bushwhacking down the backside of the summit ridge, Nora finally found her pack. It was right where she'd left it at the foot of the summit. The squirrels had chewed a hole through the bottom and gotten into her food supply. The peanuts were gone, but they'd left the candy bars alone. Nora redistributed her mom's ashes and the contents of the daypack into her large blue backpack. She placed the handgun into the top compartment next to the topo map.

According to her map, Nora had to descend the mountain's south side in order to find the ranch and hopefully the Chapel of the Sacred Heart. In some places, the trees and scrub brush were so thick that she had to fight for each step down the mountain. After an hour of battling through trailess scrub to the bottom, Nora found an opening in the trees where she was able to see the central valley of the island below her. Her face and arms were covered with red welts left by the branches that had reluctantly let her pass down the mountain. A dirt road, wide enough for a single vehicle, ran the length of the valley below. To the west, the road led to the sea. The ranch must lie to the east.

It was dark when Nora came upon the ranch. There were lights burning in the main ranch house with several jeeps parked in front. She crouched down next to an older model jeep that looked as if it had been driven through mud and listened to the voices inside of the house. There seemed to be at least one woman talking among men. Maybe if they were preoccupied, she could go about searching for the chapel without being discovered.

Clouds blanketed the sky, blocking any light from the moon, but she could still make out the shapes of the other ranch buildings in the darkness. Which of these was the Chapel of the Sacred Heart? Nora walked towards the first building, a large barn. A corral fence ran several hundred feet into a field from the barn. Nora followed the fence until she heard the winnowing of horses somewhere ahead of her. At this rate, it might take her all night to find the chapel. And even if she found it, she didn't know where she would bury her mom's ashes.

Nora decided to put off finding the chapel until morning. She ran the risk of being run off the ranch in the light of day, but at least she would get a good look at the chapel that her mom had loved so much. Nora came to a small shed, and finding the door unlocked, went inside. It smelled of oil, like the maintenance building at the marina where she had stolen the bolt cutters. Nora felt for the flashlight that she'd put in the top pocket of her pack.

It felt strange running her hand over the cold steel of the gun that was there also. Her eyes fell on a dark shadow at one end of the room. Whatever it was, it wasn't moving. Her breath hitched and she clicked on her flashlight. Someone had stacked seed bags against the wall. In one corner was a desk with a file cabinet that looked like it was used as a worktable. On it were coffee cans that contained loose machine parts. In the corner opposite the desk was a collection of rakes, shovels and gardening spades. Nora quietly moved the equipment out of the way to make room for her sleeping bag.

Even though she had been going non-stop since before first light and was bone-tired, she couldn't imagine falling asleep in such a grungy place. Nora rolled out her sleeping bag out in the corner. Before she slept, she prayed quietly. She had prayed very little since her problems had begun a few weeks ago. And this was odd for her, a pastor's daughter, who had been praying daily since she could speak.

"God, please forgive me for stealing the sailboat. And please forgive me for hating my dad." Nora closed her eyes.

She heard the skittering of mice feet. When she was almost asleep, she murmured another prayer. "Protect Brian. It's my fault if he gets hurt. Amen."

Chapter 36

Nora woke before the sun. She was stiff from lying on the cement floor of the shed and had to go to the bathroom. The thought of getting out of her warm sleeping bag and going outside stopped her from moving. From where she lay, she watched the sky turn from dark to dusty gray outside the single-paned window. It was light enough to see the chapel.

Nora slid out of the sleeping bag and put on her running shoes. Outside, early morning light revealed fields that led down to the flat part of a valley where the ranch buildings clustered like friends. The shed where she had spent the night stood alone on the side of a hill. In the field before her, long rows of leafy vegetables grew, and next to it was a pasture for the grazing animals.

Then she saw the steeply pitched roof of the chapel. Nora returned to the shed. She pulled the metal box containing her mom's ashes from her pack. She opened the lid to the box one more time and ran her finger through the fine ash. This was Sarah, she thought; this was Mom.

Wasting no time, Nora took the ashes and the small camp shovel and hurried across the field towards the chapel. The Chapel of the Sacred Heart was a small one-room red brick church surrounded by a white picket fence. A small cemetery lay directly behind the chapel. Nora tried the door and it was open. Inside, early morning light illuminated four stained glass windows along opposite walls.

An altar with a hand-carved crucifix graced the front of the chapel. Nora sat down in one of seats facing the altar, imagining her young mother sitting in this same place many years ago. The call of two scrub jays in the oak tree outside the chapel interrupted the silence.

"This is it, Lord." Nora closed her eyes and murmured a prayer.

Nora could have sat there forever, but she knew if she wanted to bury her mom's ashes she needed to get started. She scouted the cemetery for an inconspicuous place. Nora walked up the hill towards the back fence of the cemetery and decided that this would be a fine place for her mom to rest. From here, she would have a view of the ranch and the surrounding mountains.

Using her camp shovel, Nora carefully cut the top layer of grass in a perfect square. She laid the pad of sod to the side and began digging. She wanted to dig down about two feet, but the ground beneath the sod was hard. Nora piled small shovelfuls of hardpan soil onto the grass. After what seemed like an hour, Nora was finally able to place the steel box containing her mom's ashes into the compact grave. She had carried Sarah's ashes for not quite a day, and already felt attached to them. It took her a moment before she could cover the gray steel box with dirt and say goodbye.

"Bye, Momma," Nora said, crying now. "I'll come visit, I promise." She quickly filled in dirt over the steel box and carefully laid the square of sod where it fit. She patted this down with the flat part of her shovel. Nora manicured the area the best that she could and sat cross-legged next to the grave looking towards the ranch house. Whatever happened now, she didn't care.

Nora returned to the gardening shed and got her backpack. When she came out, a woman in uniform stood outside the door. Although she didn't have a mirror, Nora imagined she looked hideous. She raked fingers through her tangled hair.

"Are you lost?" the ranger asked. A radio hung from her belt.

"Just checking out the ranch," Nora said, trying not to look at the chapel.

"You realize you're trespassing?" The ranger unclasped the strap covering the radio.

"I didn't know. My boyfriend dropped me off at the beach so I could go hiking and I ended up here." Nora threw her arm in the direction of the barn.

"Did he drop you at Prisoner's Cove?" the ranger asked.

"Yeah, that's where I'm supposed to meet him," Nora lied.

"The road's that way." The ranger pointed a bony finger beyond the ranch house. Then she dropped her arm. "Do you need a ride?"

"No thanks," Nora said. She hooked her thumbs behind the shoulder straps of her pack and started walking. She felt the eyes of the ranger on her back. She hiked past the ranch house and followed a tire-rutted road through a stand of eucalyptus trees. After jogging most of the way, Nora came in view of Prisoner's Harbor. The old road led right to the end of a pier.

Nora ran to the end of the old wooden structure and peered over the railing. She took off her pack and set it down beside her. She looked west up the coast hoping to catch site of Brian and the sailboat, but saw only rocky coastline. Whitecaps churned offshore.

"Brian, where are you?" A dizzying spike of anxiety stabbed at her brain, threatening to topple her off the pier. The muscles in her stomach tightened as if to fend off a blow.

"Not now!" Nora's knees buckled and she sat down hard.

She rifled through her pack until she found the map of the island. She smoothed it out on the weathered boards. She put a finger on Prisoners and the other where she thought Lady's should be. She looked up at the mountain ridge she'd traversed the day before. Too far to go back the way she'd come. Her mind spun. What if Brian died because of her?

A cold gust sent the map fluttering into the sea.

Where were her meds? She yanked the pill bottle from her pack. "No!" She shook her head.

She would do this with a clear head. Nora opened the bottle and turned it upside down. Rose-colored tablets spilled between her dangling feet into the waves below.

She felt an eruption of emotion well up in her throat. "No more meds, Mom!"

She slung the bottle seaward and watched it disappear beneath the waves.

Chapter 37

Nate awoke to waves pounding against the hull. He looked at the green dial of his watch. It was 3 a.m. *No Worries* lurched against her anchor. Nate groped for his flashlight. Rigging clanged above him. He stuck his head through the open hatch. A cold breeze hit him in the face like a bucket of ice water. *No Worries* had swung on her anchor one hundred and eighty degrees. If she dragged anchor, he'd end up on the rocky beach.

Feeling blindly for the companionway steps, Nate climbed on deck. Fog left the boat slippery with dew. He clung to the lifelines. *No Worries* strained against her anchor. Nate stared into the dark sea. Phosphorescence sprinkled white light each time the line pulled taut. Just hold until morning, he thought. A cold gust whistled in the spreaders above him. Nate smelled the metallic wetness of an oncoming storm. He went below and crawled into the v-berth. He clasped his hands beneath his chin. "Please God, just let my anchor hold."

***

Nate woke to the coffee pot slamming onto the cabin floor. He jumped up and peered out the cabin window. The gray sea was awash in whitecaps. He felt cold coffee run between his toes before draining beneath the floorboards. Better coffee than seawater, he thought. Then, a jolt of fear seized him- *what if the storm slammed him against the rocks and he sank No Worries?*

The VHF radio crackled to life.

"U.S. Coastguard, this is sailing vessel Blue calling for assistance ..."

Nate cranked up the volume. He recognized the voice as Brian's, the kid from the docks.

"Location is Lady's Anchorage, Santa Cruz Island." Brian said.

The Coast Guard operator replied. *"Put on your lifejacket, Blue, and stay with your vessel."*

"Got to get moving!" Nate stumbled on deck to start the engine. He figured he was two hours from Lady's depending on the wind.

Nate ran forward to pull anchor. Once it was stowed, he leapt behind the wheel and pointed the sailboat towards open ocean, making headway to Lady's.

Nate twisted the wheel lock tightly and went below. He grabbed the handset to the radio. "This is sailing vessel *No Worries* calling *Blue,* over." Nate repeated the call and waited.

"This is sailing vessel Blue."

As he'd heard other mariners do, Nate said, "*Blue,* switch to channel twenty-five."

Nate switched channels and waited.

"No Worries this is Blue," Brian said.

"Brian, is that you? This is Nate Prichard!" Nate said into his mike.

"Yeah, it's me."

"Hey man, I'm on my way from Chinese harbor right now. Can you hold on?" Nate said.

"Might be on the rocks by then. Getting blown on a lee shore without an engine. Anchor's no good."

"Hang in there, buddy. Be there as soon as I can," Nate said, over the drone of his engine.

"I'll stand by on channel sixteen," Brian said.

"Copy that, *No Worries* out."

Nate heard another voice boom over the static. *"Blue, can you hear me?"*

He swore it sounded like Nora's dad. Just as he picked up the radio's handset, the boat was knocked down. Green sea poured down the companionway steps. Drenched, Nate clambered on deck as the boat righted itself. He slammed a shoulder into the cockpit floor and found himself looking up at tattered sailcloth. The knockdown had shredded his mainsail.

Clouds boiled black over the island. Back at the wheel, Nate brought the sailboat within two hundred yards of shore where the water was calmer. Someone waved to him from Prisoner's Pier. He knew the island tourists met their charter boats at the pier.

Nate focused his binoculars and thought he recognized Nora.

"I can't believe this!" Nate said.

He steered for the pier.

Within shouting distance, Nate raised cupped hands to his mouth, "What are you doing out here!?"

Nora motioned for him to bring the boat in. The wind swell was strong enough that it would smash *No Worries* against the pier if he got too close. Nate saw a boarding ladder between the pilings. He managed to steer *No Worries'* bow beneath it. Nora shouldered her pack and climbed down the old ladder that stopped short above the water.

Nora shouted, "I'll jump!"

"Wait!" he yelled. With the heavy pack, she'd go straight to the bottom if she missed.

Nora leapt four feet from the last rung of the rusty ladder. Her feet made a loud thump on the cabin top.

Jamming down on the throttle, Nate reversed away from the pier before the boat slammed into the pilings.

"Nate, thank God! I need to find Brian."

"He's at Lady's." He spun the wheel, setting the boat back on course.

Nora steadied herself against the mast as she shed her backpack.

"Brian's in trouble," Nate said. "Just spoke with him on the radio. No engine and his anchor isn't holding."

Nora's smile disappeared. She fixed her gaze on the island. "This is my fault."

"Blaming yourself isn't going to help him. Why you out here?"

"I came to the island two days ago to bury my mom," she said.

Maybe she'd gone crazy, he thought. "Your mom's been dead for what, ten years?"

She stared blankly at the churning sea. "I found her ashes buried on that ridge." She pointed to the cloud-covered mountains beyond the beach. "I brought them down to the ranch and buried them." Her face hardened. "I found this."

She unzipped the top pocket of her pack and removed a gun. She shoved it in the waistband of her jeans before stumbling across the rolling deck. She wrapped her arms around Nate. "Thanks for rescuing me."

Nate felt the butt end of her gun dig into his hip.

"You're welcome." He hugged her with his free arm while he steered the sailboat. "That thing loaded?"

"My guess is there's one bullet in it."

"Why don't you let me stow it."

Nora handed him the gun. He slid it into a compartment behind the wheel.

"So Brian sailed you out here?" Nate asked.

"Yeah, on an abandoned boat we found locked up at the marina," Nora said. "He stayed aboard while I went ashore to find my mom." Nora explained the story from the beginning. She described in detail how she had found her dad's journal and how that led her to the island.

"Incredible, huh?" Nora asked.

He nodded.

"I buried her." Nora's voice trailed off. She leaned her head on Nate's shoulder. "My dad was going to blow his head off with that gun."

"Hans, suicide? No way!"

She barely nodded. "He left a note."

Nate recognized her river of despair and didn't shy away. He pulled her close. Nora brushed his face with hers.

He lifted her chin and found her lips. Something he'd wanted to do for a long time. "I love you," he said.

She wiped away a tear.

A wave slammed against the port side, drenching them both.

The wind howled at twenty-five knots. White caps rose like demons from the green sea and drove the sailboat back. Pushed to its limit, the diesel engine drummed beneath the cockpit floor.

Nora put her hand on the wheel. "Can it go faster?"

The boat rolled. Nate braced himself, holding them both. "She's maxed out."

Together they gripped the wheel. Nora pulled her wind-whipped hair from her face and twisted it into a bun behind her head. Her tanned skin glistened with tiny water droplets, reminding Nate of the last time they'd surfed The Point. With her chin tilted upward, she appeared to be challenging the storm.

No Worries plunged into the trough of a wave. Deck awash, the lifeline tore loose from its stanchion posts.

"Nate!" Nora screamed. She pitched headlong against the starboard rail. The mangled lifeline gave beneath her weight. Her foot caught on a cleat. She hung over the side of the boat. Jagged waves ripped at Nora, as if to drag her into the sea.

Nate grabbed her ankles with both hands. The boat rounded up into the wind. He managed to pull her back into the cockpit. She fell into his arms. They kissed.

He brushed her hair back away from her face and saw the terror in her eyes. "You okay?"

She nodded, then shook her head. "No."

Chapter 38

"There he is!"

No Worries closed to within one hundred yards of the capsized *Blue*. Brian struggled to hang on to the upturned keel.

Nora stood drenched in the bow pulpit at the ready. Like a cat ready to spring, she wanted to swim for Brian.

Nate yelled, "Fifteen feet! Too shallow!" He backed down on the throttle.

"Nora, I need your help." Nate had gathered all of the life jackets in the cockpit.

Having her own rescue plan, Nora unfastened the gaskets that held Jacob's longboard.

"Only way to save him is with the surfboard!" Brian was on the rocks because of her. She lifted the board over her head.

"No! Throw lifejackets!" Nate commanded. The anchorage was completely blown out. White-capped waves beat against the hull of *Blue*. She lost sight of Brian.

Nora pointed the board at *Blue*. A wave punched into the starboard side. Nora crashed to the deck. The longboard tumbled into the water.

"Stop the boat!" Nora scrambled to her feet and watched the surfboard drift astern.

She shucked off her jacket.

"No!" Nate screamed.

Nora leapt into the roiling sea. Arm over arm, she swam against the sea. The waves fought back. Her mouth filled with water. She struggled for air.

Nate slowed the sailboat and made a tight turn towards her.

"Swim to the boat!" he shouted.

Nora swam for the longboard. She managed to snag it. She hoisted herself on the board and paddled for the overturned *Blue*. "Brian!" she screamed.

Nate cut her off. The longboard rammed into *No Worries'* port side.

"What the heck you doing!" Nate extended his hand.

Nora persisted. "I can paddle from here," she shouted over the wind. "I can save him!"

"Get on the boat!" Nate demanded. He struggled to hold on to her without tumbling overboard himself.

Nora hoisted herself up onto the swim step. She stumbled to her feet, refusing to take Nate's hand.

"You could have killed yourself!" Nate caught her by the arm as she climbed into the cockpit.

"In case you hadn't noticed, Brian's drowning!"

Brian waved frantically.

"I'll try to get as close as I can, then throw the lifejackets." He turned to Nora. "Be ready to pull him in.

If he can get a hold of a life jacket, he should be able to swim to us."

Nora could see that Brian had stopped struggling to hang on. He drifted away from the overturned boat.

Nate pulled *No Worries* to within ten yards of *Blue*.

Nora heaved every life jacket on board at Brian, but he didn't swim for them.

Nora cupped her hands to her mouth and shouted, "Grab a jacket! Swim!"

The waves pushed over Brian's shoulders and covered his head. He appeared to be looking for something below the surface. "Brian!" Nora shouted again, "Swim!"

Strong gusts pushed *No Worries* closer to the rocks. Nate had to circle out again. Nora clenched the stern rail. She wanted to jump.

"Don't lose sight of him!" Nate screamed.

"There he is!" Nora's eyes locked onto the spot behind a wave.

Nate made a pass to within twenty feet of Brian.

Barely audible, Brian yelled, "Shark!" and disappeared.

Nora recognized the unmistakable dorsal fin. The shark swam about ten feet from *No Worries'* starboard side. It was headed towards Brian.

Nora grabbed Jacob's longboard from the cabin top. She launched, board and all, into the churning sea.

The nine-foot surfboard bounced atop the white caps, but Nora managed to stay on. When she got to Brian, she slipped off the board and dropped below the surface. She found him suspended underwater. He looked to be free falling through the darkness. She grabbed him beneath the arms. Nora kicked to the surface.

"Brian, for God's sake, breathe! I can't hold you!"

Brian didn't respond. With strength that she didn't think she had, Nora got him onto the longboard. She climbed up behind him. She turned the board and paddled. Twenty yards to the safety of *No Worries*. Behind her, waves crashed against the rocks. It would be suicide to go ashore. Nora put her head down and paddled for Nate.

A steel-hulled fishing boat came into the cove from the north. Its bow bled streaks of rust. Nora thought she saw her dad standing amidst lobster traps on the stern. "Lord! What's he doing here!"

Within a few feet of reaching *No Worries*, Nora looked into Nate's eyes.

"Nora, you can make it!" he screamed.

Brian's dead weight drove the board's nose beneath the waves. She kicked furiously. Then, she felt it, a terrible jerk on her left leg. In what seemed like slow motion, the submarine-sized shark swam past her, brushing her arm with its sandpaper-like skin. Its tail slapped Nora in the side of the head. Stunned and bleeding, she ceased paddling.

The lobster fishing boat swung its stern within inches of *No Worries*. As if in a dream, Nora watched her dad dive from atop a lobster trap. He swam to her.

Although Nora saw his lips move, she couldn't hear what he said. Only the hollow sound of the ocean reverberated inside her head, much like when she'd put her ear against a seashell when she was a little girl. She knew she would probably die, but keeping her eyes on her dad gave her reason enough not to slip off the board. She looked up to see Nate at the wheel. He pointed the black muzzle of the handgun in their direction. The pistol's muzzle flashed yellow again and again. More than one bullet, she thought.

The last thing Nora saw was the look in her dad's eyes when he pushed her surfboard towards *No Worries*. No terror, but confidence. It was the same look of assuredness that she remembered when he baptized new believers at The Point. His mouth moved, but without sound. "You'll be okay."

Her dad put his head down and stroked hard in the opposite direction. He swam towards the shark. Its steel gray fin traced a jagged line on the surface. Then, the shark's circle tightened around her dad. She looked away and then he was gone. Nora's vision turned sideways and she felt warmth flow up her body into her chest.

Before she lost consciousness, Nora felt someone cradle her against the violent jarring of the sailboat. He had propped her head up using his jacket. She heard his voice.

"Please God, save her." It was Nate. He placed a small medallion around her neck, laying it next to her mom's silver cross.

She lay on the cockpit floor of *No Worries* awash in seawater and her own blood. For a moment, she fought the urge to sleep. Behind Nate stood her dad and a woman with a wonderful smile. How could they be happy at a time like this, she thought. Then she knew.

"Momma? Daddy?" Nora mouthed the words. Her mom and dad knelt down, cradling her in their arms, telling her everything would be okay. And the words to her mom's favorite gospel played softly in her head.

"In every high and stormy gale,

My anchor holds within the veil.

On Christ the solid Rock I stand,
All other ground is sinking sand;
All other ground is sinking sand."

Chapter 39

Four months later.

Orange flakes of rust fluttered into the sea as Nate climbed the ancient boarding ladder. Grandpa Jack steadied the new inflatable beneath Prisoner's Harbor pier. The calm Pacific reflected the crystalline sky like a silver dollar. They were going ashore at Santa Cruz Island.

"Can you tie us off?" Nate handed the bowline to Grandpa Jack.

A rucksack slung from his shoulder, Nate climbed onto the pier. Grandpa Jack handed him the shovel and followed him up.

"Think they had a problem?" Nate asked.

Nora had been living with her grandparents since she got out of the hospital. He'd picked her up that morning in Camarillo and brought her to Ventura Harbor for the ride to the island.

"Lobster Bob said he'd be right behind us."

Lobster fisherman Bob had offered to bring Nora and Grandma Louise to the island on his fishing boat. Neither wanted to step foot on his sailboat.

Nate heard the steady thump of Lobster Bob's diesel engine before he saw him round around the point. Bob was in the wheelhouse waving his fingerless hand. Nora, her blond hair tied back with her mom's tangerine-colored headscarf, stood in the stern with his grandmother. Nate had gone to the Surfers Church and found the boxes containing her mom's things. He brought them to Nora in the hospital. She had worn one of her mom's headscarves every day while she healed.

Bob maneuvered his stern beneath the boarding ladder and Nate helped his grandma and Nora onto the pier.

A female ranger met them on the pier, welcoming them to the island.

"Thanks for this, Nate." Nora kissed Nate on the cheek. She entwined her hand with his. Her mom's silver cross and the Saint Christopher's medal lay against her tanned skin.

Nate looked down at Nora's new prosthetic leg. Her right leg was tanned and strong while her left was a lightweight titanium bar that started below the knee. The foot was covered with a running shoe. Thanks to Nate, she had only lost her leg. After pulling her into the sailboat behind Brian, Nate took the leash from his dad's old longboard and cinched the tourniquet that saved her life.

Brian had survived too, but Nora's dad wasn't so lucky. Lobster Bob had fished his shark bitten body from the roiling ocean. He was dead before Bob got him on deck. Coast Guard swimmers had lifted Nora in a basket to their helicopter.

Nate kissed Nora and picked up the rest of their things from the dock.

Nora stumbled, and then quickly regained her balance. "I'm still getting used to this thing." She hopped ahead of him to walk with Nate's grandparents to an awaiting jeep. The royal treatment from the island ranger was probably due to the immense media coverage over the shark attack. Nate had been on every news show for a week after the accident. One network even flew him to New York.

"Understand you've been given permission to bury some ashes in the cemetery today," the ranger said.

"Yes, Nora has," Nate replied.

"Then I'll take you to the Chapel."

"Any problems crossing the channel?" the ranger asked.

"Nope, it was smooth as glass," Grandpa said.

"Great day to be on the water," Nate said. Grandma and Nora nodded in agreement. It was the first time Nate had sailed since the accident. But that wasn't the reason. He just hadn't wanted to leave Nora. He stood by her every step of the way through the huge memorial service for Hans and the long weeks of physical therapy since the doctors released her from the hospital.

"Nate, I want things to be the same." Nora cried softly and put her head against his shoulder. Grandma Louise stroked her hair.

"Yeah, I know." But he knew she would never see the world the same again. The tragedy of losing her dad and then her leg to the shark would forever color every remaining moment of her life.

The ranger parked her jeep in front of the Chapel of the Sacred Heart.

Nora led the way behind the chapel to finish what she had come to the island to do.

When the Coast Guard helicopter landed at the hospital, the emergency room doctors were surprised Nora was still alive. Maybe she'd held on that long because she was so determined to see the chapel again.

"I took my mom from Devil's Peak and put her by the Sacred Heart." She had told the doctors this before they wheeled her into surgery. They didn't know what she was talking about until Nate explained later how she had come to the island to find her mom's ashes.

Nora came to a place along the cemetery fence where the ground was sunken. Not able to bend her prosthetic leg, she dropped to the grass. "This is the place," she said.

Nate took the shovel and removed a perfect square of green sod. The soil turned easily under the shovel's blade. Nora had done the hard digging months ago when she was here. He removed scoops of dirt until the shovel blade struck the old metal box that she had told him about.

Nora brushed dirt from around the handle and lifted the gunmetal box from the shallow grave.

"Hi Mom, I've come to say goodbye again." She opened the lid and gently ran a finger through the fine ash.

Nate pulled a larger hand-carved mahogany box from his rucksack and set it on the ground next to Nora. Inside were the ashes of her dad.

Nora carefully poured her mom's ashes into the mahogany box, joining them with her dad's. She closed the lid and fastened the copper clasp on its front. Tears welled in her eyes as she placed the wooden box back into the shallow grave. She wiped her eyes with the corner of her headscarf.

Nate pushed a shovelful of dirt into the hole.

"That's okay." Nora gently pushed the shovel blade away and scooped handfuls of dirt over the burnished box.

When Nora had filled in the grave, she replaced the square of sod. She positioned a brass plaque engraved with her parents' names in the grass. The ranger had told them she would take care of anchoring the plaque in place later with a small headstone.

Nora stood up the best she could and brushed dirt from her khaki shorts. "They're home now, forever," she said. She'd said the same at her dad's memorial service. Nora had given the eulogy. Her vision of her parents together in heaven was spoken with such eloquence that God Himself might have prepared her notes.

Nora took Nate's hand as they walked out the gate of the cemetery. She turned to him. "I'll never leave you," she said.

He stopped and ran his finger along the gentle curve of her jaw, studying the contours of her face like a map. Even though the storms they'd weathered had irrevocably changed each of them, Nate knew the tragic events would bind him to Nora forever. He kissed her softly and hoped for something poetic. Clearing his throat, he said, "You are the ocean and I am the shore."

"That's deep." She managed a laugh and tousled his hair.

Nate looked over at his grandparents who sat arm in arm on the steps of the chapel. Grandpa Jack nodded and stood up, holding out his hand to Grandma Louise.

Nora's good leg buckled beneath her. He caught her by the arm before she could fall.

"You okay?" he asked.

"Yeah, I can do this." She picked up the shovel and used it as a walking stick. She hopped down the tire-rutted road from which they came. She looked over her shoulder. "You guys, I'm going to walk back."

Nate grabbed the rucksack and jogged to catch up with her.

"Think we can see Surfers Point from the pier?" she asked.

Nate thought about it for a moment. "Bet you're right."

She took his hand. When they came to a crest in the road, they saw the Santa Barbara Channel spread out before them, a vast plain of blue.

Nora leaned on the shovel. "There it is." She pointed.

He nodded and squinted at the cloudless horizon. Beneath the coastal mountains on the far side of the channel, he thought he saw a wave breaking at The Point.

The End

Author's Note

Surfer's Point in Ventura is one of the best surf breaks in Southern California. On a clear day, if you look beyond the waves at The Point, you can see Picacho Diablo, or Devil's Peak, the highest mountain on Santa Cruz Island. The eastern end of the island is part of the Channel Islands National Park and can be visited by anyone willing to endure the twenty-mile boat ride from the mainland.

John Erickson

Made in the USA
Las Vegas, NV
15 January 2021